TALES from the ARENA
OPENING GAMBIT

Elizabeth Schechter

Circlet
Press

Also by Elizabeth Schechter:
Chains of Light
Fools Rush In
Heart's Master
Her Captive
House of Sable Locks
Princes of Air
The Rebel Mage Series

Opening Gambit © 2018 by Elizabeth Schechter
Previously published as Tales from the Arena: Opening Gambit

Cover credits:
Female figure © Yurmary | fotosearch.com
Background art © Algolonline | fotosearch.com

ISBN 978-1-61390-198-4 paperback
Also available in digital formats.

Circlet Press, Inc.
39 Hurlbut Street
Cambridge, MA 02138

www.circlet.com

Prologue

"What are we supposed to *do* with them?"

The question echoed in the cavernous university lecture hall that had been acting as the ersatz Council chamber ever since the bombing of Amali City, the capital of Tyese. No one answered. Andradae looked around at her fellow Council members and sighed, fighting the urge to rub her temples as her headache grew. When she'd volunteered for the Council, she'd never expected to become Senior Councilor. Damn the Aakari, and the bombs that had killed most of the Ruling Council in Amali. Ten years, and still no end in sight—

"Pardon, Councilor, but did you mean the researchers? Or the... soldiers?" someone asked. Andradae didn't recognize the voice. One of the newer Council members, she assumed.

"Both," Andradae answered. "They're heroes, the lot of them. They've saved countless lives, not to mention the entire Tyesean nation. They won the war. More importantly, they ended the war! And... they're illegal. So, the question remains: what do we do with them?"

As if on cue, the doors at the rear of the hall swung open, and into the chamber marched a dozen black-clad men and women, accompanied by two men wearing the white and red coveralls of the medical research college.

Andradae rose. "What is the meaning of this?" she demanded.

One man in black stepped forward and bowed. "I ask the Council's indulgence. My brothers- and sisters-in-arms have asked me to speak for them. I am Quaran, Ran-ti-ar of the Ishkarin."

"Ish—" Andradae blinked. "That's Old Tyesean."

Quaran almost hid his smile. "Yes, Senior Councilor. I am—I was—a linguist, before I volunteered." He looked around, and Andradae was struck by his calm demeanor and the intelligence in his dark

3

eyes. He was older than she originally thought—this close, she could see the silver at his temples, and the wrinkles around his eyes.

"I see," Andradae said slowly. "And it means?"

The smile was definitely visible now. "It means Black Sword, Councilor."

"Thank you," Andradae said with a smile. "You've come to speak to the Council. The Council is listening."

Quaran bowed again and clasped his hands behind his back. "Thank you. Councilors. I am Ran-ti-ar. That is, I am the acknowledged leader of the Ishkarin. And I come to you to with a request, and with a proposal."

"Why do you think you have the right to come to us and ask anything?"

Andradae gasped at the hateful tone of Under-Secretary Durrant's voice, but Quaran merely looked amused by the question. "I am Quaran. I am a son of Tyese, a son of this very city, as are you, I think, Councilor Durrant?" He didn't wait for an answer, looking at the rest of the Councilors. "I am as you are, save in only one area. You did not ask to be born. I did. We all did, my brethren and I. We volunteered for our new lives. We gave up our families, our careers, our castes, so that we could become something more, and serve Tyese."

"You did," Andradae said. "You did, and we are all grateful. But your purpose is now served."

"And that is why we've come. Our purpose is served," Quaran agreed. "The war is over. But we face the aftermath now, and the question of what is to be done with the Ishkarin must be answered."

Andradae nodded. "And... I presume you have an answer?"

"One possible answer, yes, Councilor," Quaran said. "On behalf of my Ishkarin, I hereby volunteer our services to the Council, and to Tyese, in perpetuity."

"Your services?" Durrant asked. "What need does the Council have for a troop of manufactured killing machines?"

"Durrant!" Andradae snapped. "That was uncalled for!"

"We've been called worse," Quaran said drily. "And, to answer the question? There have been no riots since the ceasefire was called. No looting. No disorder. Not here, nor in Aakar." He fell silent, and smiled.

"Malena?" Andradae asked without turning. "Is that true?"

"It is, Senior Councilor. And frankly, we've been wondering why. It's... not the norm," Malena answered, and Andradae heard soft beeping coming from Malena's datapad. "Every time we've had a break in the fighting before, the damage from... call it friendly fire, was worse than what we'd had from across the Melnamore."

Andradae nodded. "Thank you, Malena. Quaran, this was your doing?"

Quaran bowed slightly. "It was, Senior Councilor. There is no point in winning a war if there is nothing to come home to. This is our proposal. That the Ishkarin become the military arm of the Council. We will maintain the law, maintain the peace, both in Tyese and in Aakar." He fell silent, and the Council members all looked at each other, their confusion plain.

Finally, Andradae cleared her throat. "Let me see if I understand you plainly," she said slowly. "You are volunteering to become... peace-keepers?"

"Yes, Senior Councilor," Quaran answered. "We feel that there would be a need, and it is the logical role for us to take. We are made for conflict, and it will be quite a few years before the people of either nation come to terms with being at peace. There will be enough for the Council to worry about without having to think of keeping order. The armies of both nations are tired, and rightfully so. To ask them to take on the role would be cruel. Let them go home."

"But, to maintain that kind of presence here and in Aakar..." Malena frowned as her voice trailed off. "Quaran, how many *are* you?"

"Our main force is made up of four hundred and thirty-five men and women, Councilor. We had some losses," Quaran answered.

"How many losses?" Andradae asked.

"Fifteen, in the final push to the Imperial compound, Councilor."

Andradae nodded, then actually heard what Quaran had said. "Your *main* force," she repeated. "That number... that isn't the total number of Black Swords, is it?"

Quaran smiled broadly, and his unassuming features were suddenly strikingly handsome. "I see why you are the Senior Councilor. No, Councilor, that is not our total number. We have twice that in training, men and women who are too young to serve at this time. And we have children—"

"You can *breed*?"

Quaran ignored the outburst from the Health Minister, a man who had nearly had apoplexy when he'd discovered what his own researchers had been doing under his nose. "— who may or may not have inherited the enhanced abilities. Time will tell."

"I see," Andradae murmured.

"Senior Councilor, may I?"

"Of course, Malena." Andradae took her seat, suddenly feeling as if she'd been standing for years. Malena rose and smiled at the Ishkarin.

"Quaran Ran-ti-ar, you said a proposal and a request. We've heard the proposal. What was the request?"

Quaran looked oddly embarrassed. He shifted slightly, from one foot to the other. It was a small movement, one barely visible, but in someone who had been standing at attention, it was startling.

"We... are hunters. Predators," Quaran answered, obviously searching for the right words. "It is what we were made to be. And... it is what we are. Our purpose was to end the war. Now, we have no purpose. It is my hope that acting a peacekeepers will fulfill some part of our... instinct. But I am afraid that it will not be enough."

"Speak clearly, Quaran," Andradae said. "What is it that you need?"

"Prey, Councilor," Quaran said, his voice flat. "We must have something on whom we can prey. We've tried mock drills, and they are not enough."

"If I may?" One of the researchers stepped forward, a tall, bony man with unwashed brown hair. "I am Brinnock. I was Researcher Mathias' assistant in his work of creating the Swords."

"Oh, good. Then you can tell us where we can find Mathias," Health Minister Lurton said.

"He's dead, Councilor," Brinnock answered. "He died in a bombing raid, last year. The one that destroyed the northern research facilities. We've continued his work, but... we none of us have his touch. And, from his notes, I can tell you that the modifications of the Black Swords was never meant to be permanent. But without Mathias, we've no hope of reversing what was done."

"And the traits breed true?" Lurton asked.

"In sixty percent of recorded cases, yes, but—"

"Wait," Lorton said, holding up one hand. "If you can cite a reliable statistical sample of how many children have inherited these abilities, this project has been going on longer than any of us thought."

Quaran nodded. "That is true, Councilor. I volunteered for the program when I was eighteen. I am now forty-one."

"Over twenty years," Andradae murmured. "Well, then, Brinnock. What can you tell us?"

"We chose the candidates for the initial test subjects based on several factors. Intelligence was one factor. Aggression was another, as was a certain... ruthlessness, I suppose you would call it. What we ended up with were soldiers who would stop at nothing to defeat their enemy. What we didn't expect was that those traits, when enhanced, would also lead to a certain..." he paused, then looked at Quaran.

"We enjoy what we do, Councilors," Quaran finished. "The hunt, and the aftermath. It is... as a drug to us. We call it the bloodlust. The only problem is that if we do not regularly experience that... release, we descend into.." he paused, frowned, then nodded. "Uncontrollable rage. Which is probably about as similar to what you would call rage as saying that your glass of water there is the Melnamore. We must have prey."

"You want us to supply you with victims?" Durrant asked, his voice spiraling up in disbelief. "Have you all gone mad?"

"Not unwilling victims!" Brinnock answered quickly. "It is... there is something that Mathias discovered, as he tested for candidates for the program. That there were some who were... well, mirrors. Exactly the opposite of what he wanted. People with incredible empathy, with a need to serve, and an odd affinity for... ah... call it adversity."

"Adversity?" Ancrade repeated, and watched as the researcher turned red to his ears.

"They... ah... they seem to... to find... stimulation in... suffering," he finally stammered. "Mathias thought that these people could be trained as... as healers of sorts. The natural complement to the Swords, if you will. These would be people who could serve in the aftermath of the war, both as the logical targets of the Ishkarin's aggression and as counselors to the men and women who had spent so many years of being on the front lines of the war. He anticipated some... aftereffects among the Swords, you see, that would need more than a physical outlet. He developed a program to test for those qualities, to train them to his purpose. And he died before we could implement that second stage of his work."

"So, what you are proposing is that we approve this... program?" Andradae asked. "Is that your request?"

"It is, Councilor," Quaran answered.

"And... that is also the reason that you want to become peace-keepers?" Andradae continued, the whole suddenly clear. "Because if the entire nation is under your protection—"

"Then perhaps I can keep my Swords from preying on the people they serve," Quaran finished, nodding. "A case, perhaps, of using wolves to guard the kine."

"Wolves who still need to hunt. I see," Andradae said, rubbing the bridge of her nose with one finger. "Thank you, Quaran. The Council will consider your request and your proposal. If I may ask, how long before your wolves need to hunt again?"

Quaran bared his teeth and Andradae blinked, startled to see the human wolf standing before her. "Soon, Councilor. There are Aakari rebels in the mountains, and I will take my troops there while we wait for your decision. If you decide against, then we will remain in the mountains. For as long as I can keep them there." He bowed. "Thank you, Councilors, for your time."

Chapter One

Five Years Later

The celebration was loud and rowdy, but remained good-natured, something that the restauranteurs appreciated when the troop of Ishkarin moved on. Gavir was highly respected among the men and women of his Division, and his recent promotion to Kian-ti-os, second only to Quaran Ran-ti-ar himself, was considered by the greatest majority of Ishkarin to have been well-deserved. When the promotion had been announced, a dozen of his troops, many of whom had served under him since he had been Division Commander of their cadet troop, had made arrangements for an evening pass. A night on the town—dinner, a show, and finishing off the night at the Arena.

"Honestly, you didn't need to do this!" Gavir shouted, laughing as two of the men towed him towards the Arena entrance.

"You've done for us, for years," Delan, his Division quarter-master, said from behind him. "Let us take care of you for once, sir."

"No sirs!" Delan protested. "Not from you lot! You call me by my name."

"Rank must be observed... sir," Delan answered. Gavir turned and saw the other Sword smirking at him.

"Delan, what are you up to?" Gavir asked, tugging his arms free and stopping just outside the Arena doors.

Delan looked at the other Swords, then nodded. "All right. We made a reservation for you tonight. Here. Now come along or you'll be late."

"A reservation? Delan, I've never needed a reservation before."

"That's because you have no taste," Delan answered, his voice tart as he repeated something that Gavir had said of himself a thousand times.

"You take the first collar that catches your eye. No, we're going to make a connoisseur out of you, Gavir. Mark me on that."

"A conn... what in the Creator's name kind of reservation did you *make*?"

"You'll see," Delan answered. Gavir snorted with amusement and let the troop steer him inside.

In the five years since the Ruling Council had agreed to the proposal set forth by Quaran, the Arena had become such a focal point that there was talk of changing the name of the very city from Niran to Arena City. Once, this building had been part of the University, home to their championship gravity-ball team. Then, after the war, it had been a refugee camp, until the Council took it over and had it renovated. Now, it was simply the Arena, home to the Tarken, the White Collars, and favored hunting ground of the Ishkarin who were not in the field.

Gavir had no idea how the Tarken were chosen, but the ones who made it through their training—something he'd been assured was every bit as grueling as Sword training—served for five years. The first hundred had been released from their collars only the previous week, rewarded for their services with high-caste status and lifetime pensions. Perhaps there was a new crop of Collared, he thought as he identified himself to the gray-clad trainee behind the desk; Gavir allowed his identichip to be scanned, then accepted the control band that the trainee locked around his wrist, waiting until it showed the green lights that meant it had synced his wrist-comp to the Arena central control computer. The others of the troop followed suit, and they headed towards the lift with more laughing and ribald jokes about Gavir's admittedly bad taste in partners.

The lift doors opened again to let them out into the Lounge. The bar area was already crowded with Ishkarin and civilians alike, sitting at tables with food or drinks, chatting in corners, or gathered near the large windows that looked down onto the Floor. Gavir wandered over and looked down, smiling as he saw the people milling around between the stations. Things weren't busy on the Floor yet—he'd have his choice of equipment. Good. His fingers curled slightly as his thoughts turned darker. The whipping cross first, perhaps. Old-fashioned, yes, but so incredibly satisfying...

"Gavir?"

Gavir heard Delan call his name, turned, and saw red. Brilliant red, the color of fresh blood. He blinked, staring at the crimson-clad woman standing in front of him. As he watched, she went to her knees, bowing her head as she said, "Kian-ti-os. I serve."

He knew who she was. Iras was one of the Hundred, and there was no one among the ranks of the Swords who didn't at least know her name. She was easily the most celebrated among the Collared, one of the few womento volunteer when the call went out, and one of only twelve who made it through training and took the collar to become a Tarken. Gavir knew of her, but he had never actually worked with her—her skills were widely in demand, and she was never available for a spur-of-the-moment assignation. There were those who called her the Queen of the Arena—as beautiful as a blade, as alluring as the bloodlust.

"Red?" Gavir looked at Delan. "Red collars?"

"Some of the Hundred chose to remain in their collars when their contracts ended," Delan answered. "The Council created a new rank for them. They're called Taramar."

Gavir nodded, walking over to slowly circle the kneeling woman. "The red suits you," he growled, feeling his blood rise as he watched the muscles of her back flex and shift under her skin as she shivered. Her dark hair was short, baring the long, graceful column of her neck, and her creamy skin was amazingly unmarked. The perfect canvas. *She must respond well to regen*, Gavir mused as he reached down to trail his fingernails over the knob of her spine, just under her collar. "Stand up, Iras. I want to see you."

She rose, crossing her wrists behind her back as Gavir walked around her once more. She was tall for a woman, almost as tall as he was, and he admired the way her long muscles wrapped around her bones, the strength in her long legs and the sweet curves of her hips and waist. He wondered what she would look like when she was screaming. He stopped in front of her and smiled. "Look at me, Iras."

She looked up, an almost insolent gleam in her startlingly pale blue eyes. There was a challenge there, and Gavir suddenly knew why she was so much in demand. There was something else, too. He looked at her, met her eyes, and asked, "What are you thinking?"

She looked startled, but recovered quickly. Had no one ever asked her that before? He arched an eyebrow when she didn't answer, and she blushed.

"I want to get the hair out of your eyes," she admitted.

It was Gavir's turn to be startled, then he laughed out loud. After a full day on duty that ended with being practically kidnapped by his men, he was well aware that his uniform was rumpled, and that his oft-times-annoying curly hair had started to escape from the heavy layer of pomade that he used to keep it under control. But no one, be they Sword or Collared, had ever commented on it before!

Amused and intrigued, he crossed his arms over his chest and nodded. "Go ahead."

She hesitated, and Gavir watched as the tip of her tongue flickered out to lick her lips. Then she stepped forward, close enough that he could smell her, the soft fragrance of her soap not quite masking the alluring oh-so-female musk and the slight hint of fear. He didn't move as she came closer still, until he could feel the heat radiating off of her body as she reached out and gently tucked back the errant lock of hair. It immediately fell back down, and she smiled.

"It has a mind of its own," she murmured.

"So do you," Gavir said. "I like that. Shall we go down?"

"May I offer you a drink first, Kian-ti-os?" she asked.

"Thank you. Perhaps after?"

"If you wish." She crossed her wrists behind her back again and raised her chin. "Will you mark me?"

"Oh, what an invitation," he said with a laugh, taking his personal sigil from his pouch. He pressed the seal to the front of her collar; when he removed it, he saw his own identicon had appeared on the small panel. She was his now.

"Gentlemen," he said, not looking away from Iras. "Thank you. For your congratulations, and for what is promising to be a most... enjoyable evening. Please, enjoy yourselves. Control?"

The Central Control computer spoke at once, *What is your will, Kian-ti-os?*

"My companions. Whatever they will have, on my account."

Acknowledged.

"Gavir, this is supposed to be your night!" Delan protested. Gavir looked at him and smiled.

"It is. And it pleases me to reward my men for their... glorious taste. And for their attempt to... educate my palate. Enjoy yourself, Delan." He looked back at Iras and nodded. "Shall we?"

She smiled back at him. "Yes, Kian-ti-os."

He touched his wrist-comp as they turned towards the lift, and heard Iras catch her breath as the magnetic beads in her wristbands activated, binding her wrists behind her back. Gavir reached out and rested his hand on the back of her neck, feeling her shiver slightly. Then she took a step closer to him, pressing in close to his side.

A very enjoyable night indeed, he thought, as he steered her towards the lift.

GAVIR GUIDED IRAS OUT of the lift and stopped, closing his eyes and letting the sounds and smells of the Arena wash over him. The screams of the Collared who were in use, the scent of synth-leather and ozone, mingled with sharp tangs of fear and lust. He hadn't been on a battlefield in months, and coming here was the closest he could come to really unleashing the beast within. He could feel his blood rising, and he stepped behind Iras and pulled her back against him.

"Tell me what you're afraid of, Iras," he growled into her ear. She whimpered softly and pulled against his grip. He could feel her shivering slightly, but she didn't answer his question.

"You'll tell me before I'm done," he assured her.

"I won't." Her voice was a bare hint of a whisper, and he laughed softly—a challenge.

"You're a delight, and I haven't even made you scream yet," he said, pushing her forward. "I was thinking of the whipping frames, but now... Oh, now I have other plans for you, my dear. For you and your lovely skin. Control!"

Acknowledged.

"Is the Easel available?"

Affirmative.

"Wonderful!"

As Gavir pushed Iras ahead of him towards the Easel, he heard a rustle of whispers following in their wake. He knew why—there were not many among the Swords who cultivated either the patience or the artistry to use the Easel. Of those few, Gavir was regarded as one of—if not the—best. It was, however, a time-consuming pastime. Not something to be indulged in when one had to be on shift in six hours' time. It had been months since he'd last done this.

By the time Gavir and Iras had reached the Easel's enclosure, word had spread and a crowd had started to gather. Gavir nodded, but his focus was solely on Iras, and her sudden, surprising hesitation.

"Have you never done this before?" he asked, touching his wrist-comp and releasing her wrists.

She shook her arms out before answering. "Not this, no. I've heard about it. Seen it done. Seen you do it, but never all of it."

"Ah. A learning experience, then," Gavir said. He smiled and held out his hand, bowing slightly. "This way, my dear."

He helped her step up into the hollow framework, telling her where to hold on while he secured her ankles in place inside the frame before attaching the leads to her anklebands. Then he stepped up in front of her and showed her the places for her hands, locking her wristbands into place as well. He jumped down and walked around the frame, nodding in satisfaction as he reached out and unfastened the catches on her belt, letting the long silk panels of her loincloth flutter to the ground. The band that crossed her breasts followed, and Gavir kicked the discarded clothing out of the way before returning to admire the pale perfection that was Iras' skin, broken only by the control bands on her arms and legs, and around her waist. Like most female Collared, she was completely hairless from the neck down, and Gavir could already smell her arousal.

"You're practically unmarked," he said, moving to the table and uncovering a jar. He picked up a brush and tucked it behind his ear as he looked at her. "Either you've been treated very gently, or you take regen better than most. Which is it?"

Her answer was the closest that Gavir had ever heard to indignant from any of the Collared. "None of the Collared are ever treated gently."

"And I'm not about to start," Gavir added with a laugh. He looked over the waiting supplies, and smiled. The Control computer had apparently made note of his preferences—there was a simple blindfold—no more than a strip of silk—waiting next to the brushes. He picked the length of cloth and stepped up onto the riser behind Iras. "You're quite lovely," he murmured into her ear as he blindfolded her. "This will only make you more beautiful." He jumped down and picked up a pot of paint.

If he had not been born to the blade, Gavir sometimes thought that he might have become an artist. The allure of paint and brush, or pen and ink, was something he found almost as enticing as the beautiful symmetry of his sword or the deadly perfection of his gun. He could, and had, gotten lost in artistic creation, experiencing an ecstatic state that he found very close to the blood fury that drove him during battle. He felt that building as he painted Iras, covering her skin with muted designs of gold and burnt umber, layering over those patterns traceries in shades of ruby and lapis. He painted her nipples midnight blue, and laid over that a pattern of silver that resembled fine lace, a pattern that he reproduced on her bare pubes. He heard her gasping as the rough brush trailed over the sensitive skin there, and leaned close to blow on the paint there, making her moan and thrust her hips forward.

"Almost finished, my dear," Gavir told her, picking up another paint pot. "Almost."

Down the line of her back, from the knob of her spine to where her hips flared and flowed down into her ass, he painted a waterfall, drawing on his memories of one that he'd seen once on patrol in the mountains. His reproduction crashed in magnificent power and fury against the painted rocks at the base of her spine, sending up sprays of foam and mist that he rendered in bright white paint, tapping the sharp bristles against her side perhaps a bit harder than was necessary. He painted faster now, urgency starting to overcome artistry. The paint was thick, and stayed wet a long time, but if the paint dried completely, he would have to start over.

Finally, he stepped back, dropping his brush onto the tray that was now littered with dirty brushes and half-filled pots of paint. There was a smattering of applause, and Gavir turned, seeing familiar faces against the outside of the enclosure. He smiled and sketched a mock bow, drawing laughter from them. Then he turned back to the frame, spinning it slowly so that Iras was on display, so that everyone could see the painted canvas that she had become from the hollow of her throat to her ankles.

"Now," Gavir said. "Now, just let me sign the painting." He picked up the control board for the frame, considered Iras for a moment, then pushed all the switches to full power. Iras shrieked, her entire body going taut as the conductive paints started to transmit an electrical charge over her skin. Gavir let her feel the full force of the charge for a count of ten, then eased the switches back down, leaving her gasping and whimpering in her bonds. "That was very nice," he murmured, touching the controls. His fingers danced over the panel, sending current racing through the different receptors embedded within the thick paint, making Iras twitch and moan and scream as she tried futilely to escape the torture device that he had laid on to her very skin.

Gavir continued until he saw the paints starting to crack and flake, breaking the circuits. With a sigh, he set the control board aside. Art was so fleeting. There was more applause, and the Swords who has assembled to watch started to wander away. Gavir ignored them, walking up to the frame and looking up at Iras, hanging limp, her forehead resting against one upstretched arm.

"You are a most magnificent canvas," Gavir told her. To his surprise, she smiled.

"... thank you... Sir."

He stepped back, amused beyond measure. Usually, at this point, his canvas would be completely incoherent, if not completely unconscious. To have one of them answer was new, and he finally understood just why this woman was so sought after.

"Control."

Acknowledged.

"Is a room available?"

Your preferred room has been reserved for your usage. Do you require assistance?

"No." Gavir answered. He shook his head and snorted. "That computer is getting too smart for its own good," he said to himself. Then he went to collect his now-limp canvas.

Usually, after using the Easel, Gavir would surrender his Collared canvas to one of the attendants, who would transport them to a room. This time, he waved the attendant off, gathering Iras in his arms. She rested her head against his chest and sighed. It was a soft, contented sound, so faint that he almost missed it, accompanied by a bare brushing of breath against his chest, and it sent a rush through him. Connoisseur indeed.

He carried Iras out of the enclosure and across the Arena, mindful of the attentions around him as people—Swords and Collared alike—stopped what they were doing and watched him go. At the far side of the Arena, a door dilated as he approached, letting him pass through and into a long corridor lined with more doors. A light was flashing over one, and he made for it.

The lights in the room came up as he entered, and the door sealed behind him. Inside, the room was similar to his quarters at the barracks, if only a little larger. A large bed dominated one side of the room, and there was a rack on the wall for weapons and to hang his uniform. His quarters didn't have the matching rack that carried a small array of whips and blades, though. Nor did he have attachment points set into his walls. Not that he hadn't considered adding them when he'd first been promoted to senior officer, and seen the lavish new quarters that were now his. It was a thought that had lasted for all of five minutes, until he reminded himself that *that* sort of play had to be confined to the Arena. No Sword was allowed to take prey off the battlefield or outside the Arena, under penalty of immediate and permanent exile, and Gavir had no wish to end his days in the internment camps among the Swords who couldn't control themselves.

He laid Iras on the bed and turned to the other feature of this room, one that he might just have added to his own quarters—the plunge. He'd discovered this particular amenity the first time he'd used the Easel, and had requested a place to clean up both himself and his Collared canvas. Since then, he'd apparently requested the room often enough that the computer had made a note of it. The deep, wide bathtub was already filled, the hot water filling the air with fragrant steam. Yes, he was definitely going to add one of these to his personal quarters, Gavir thought as he started to strip off his uniform.

On the bed, Iras hadn't moved since he'd laid her down. Her regular, deep breathing showed that she was asleep, and Gavir wondered at that—how could she sleep, with the amount of pain that she must be in? He knew what he'd find under the layers of paint. There would be electrical burns, possibly nasty ones. Aftercare was not usually the role of the Swords, not here in the Arena. Injured Collared were supposed to be surrendered to the medics. But he'd set his own protocols when he'd started using the Easel—he made certain that his canvases were taken care of, that all of the paint was carefully removed before he gave them up. Hence the plunge. Naked, Gavir went to the bed and carefully removed the blindfold. She was indeed asleep, but she woke up and groaned softly as he picked her up.

"What? Where are we?" She put her arms around his neck as he carried her to the plunge. "When did we get here?"

"Hush, my dear," Gavir told her as he slowly stepped down into the water, being careful not to slip on the textured tiles. "You're amazing. Do you know how amazing you are?"

She blushed prettily. "Everyone says so."

He stopped, the water lapping at his hips, washing over his erect cock. "But you don't agree?"

"Amazing? Hardly. I'm just me. What are you doing?" She looked around. "A bath?"

"The paint needs to come off, and your burns need to be seen to," Gavir explained. He took the next step down, then tightened his grip around her as he dunked them both under the hot water. She hissed at the touch of hot water on sensitive skin, her arms around his neck tightening.

"Can you stand?" Gavir asked, standing up in the now waist-deep water. "There's a seat, if you need it."

"I can stand. If you put me down." Gavir grinned and let her stand, steadying her as she wobbled on her feet. She braced herself with one hand against his bare chest, watching as colors slowly stained the water with a mixed, muted rainbow. "That was extraordinary," she said. "I see why you're so highly regarded."

"Am I?" Gavir asked, picking up a handful of water and letting it dribble from his fingers over Iras' back. The red, raw skin underneath was being to show through the thinning layers of paint.

"The Collared say you have a... what did I hear? Oh. Delicate savagery. That was it." Iras looked back at him over her shoulder. "I wasn't certain what they meant, until now."

"And what do they mean?" Gavir asked, tossing his head to get his damp hair out of his eyes. Iras giggled and turned so that she could brush it back, her wet fingers trailing over Gavir's forehead. Then she looked thoughtful, tapping her fingertips against her lip.

"Most of the Swords want to either give us pain, or they want us to take their pain. Which makes sense, really. It's what we do—"

"And you do it remarkably well," Gavir interrupted. "I've never had a conversation with someone fresh off the Easel before."

"I have an unusually high pain threshold." Iras dismissed her tolerances with a wave of her hand. "And I'm ignoring the worst of it. We're trained to do that. You... You use the pain as an accent. I heard you when you said you had to sign the canvas, right before you made me scream. It was almost as if you weren't after the pain, either the giving or the receiving. You were after the artistry of it. That makes a difference."

"Turn around and let me wash your back." Gavir considered what she'd said as he gently sponged the paint from her skin. "How so?"

"Anyone can make us scream, Gavir," Iras said over her shoulder. "You made me more than my pain and my reaction to that pain. You made me special."

Gavir stopped with the sponge resting on her shoulder. "You're not? Because I've always thought that all of you were special."

"And that is why the Collared all think so highly of you," Iras said. "You see us as special, not just as prey, or as a body to hurt. Every single Collared that you've had wants to be there when you come in, because you might choose them again. You have quite a following, Kian-ti-os."

Gavir blinked, letting the sponge fall into the water with a 'plop'. "I never knew. I thought I always saw the same faces because I always came at the last minute, and..." His voice trailed off. There was really no delicate way of saying what he was thinking. He cleared his throat. "Turn around. Let me see if I've gotten all the paint off."

She turned, raising her arms to show skin that was free of paint, and crosshatched in livid red burns and raw skin. Gavir smiled and ran one hand down her side, making her hiss once more.

"Ready to get out? There's a salve I can put on these until the medics can see to you."

She looked stunned. "That part is true, too?"

"What part?"

"That you don't use the ones off the Easel for sex? I never thought that those tales were true. But—" Iras closed her mouth with a snap, but not before Gavir caught a glimpse of something in her eyes. Her next words confirmed it, "Do you not want me?"

"Oh, Iras. I do want you. I think that is fairly clear." He looked down at himself, at his still-hard cock. "It sounds like you talk, all of you Collared. So what have you heard of me?"

"Of course we talk," she said slowly. "But..."

"What have you heard about me?" Gavir repeated.

"That you use us in the Arena, on the Floor, but if you use us on the Easel, then you won't in the bedrooms. But that is—"

"The truth." Gavir leaned back against the edge of the plunge, crossing his arms over his chest. "I don't mix my pleasures, Iras. And I won't torture you more than necessary. You'll see the medics tonight. Tomorrow, or the next day, I'll come back—"

"I won't be medically cleared for the Floor tomorrow!"

"So I'll take you to dinner," Gavir said with a smile. "Then, perhaps, I'll take you back to my quarters, and take you to bed. If you want."

She blinked. "I... don't understand you at all. You are nothing like any Sword I have ever met before, and I thought I'd seen all of them."

Gavir looked down at the water and sighed. That again. Damn it. After all this time, all his work, people could still see it? He shook his head. "Look. If this... is not acceptable to you, then I don't have to come back. I won't ask for you again. Just let me say that I've enjoyed you greatly, Iras. Enough that I would like to sleep with you. I think you're glorious. But—" His voice trailed off as he saw the look Iras was giving him. An intense, thoughtful one, that seemed to gaze right through him. Iras just looked at him like that for a long moment. She licked her lips, then came towards him, the water trailing in her wake until she stood in front of him. She said nothing, simply took his face between her hands and kissed him, pressing her long body against his and pinning him against the side of the plunge. He grabbed her arms and pushed her back.

"Iras!"

"Shut up, Gavir," she said firmly.

"I don't want to hurt you, Iras—" Gavir stopped, then smiled, laughing ruefully at his own words. "Listen to me. I sound like... such an idiot."

"You sound wonderful. That is the reason, the only reason, why you won't have me now?"

He met her eyes and smiled. "Exactly. Be patient, Iras. In a day or two? I'll make the appointment before I leave. I've seen you scream in pain, my beautiful Iras. When I come back, I want to see you scream in joy."

She licked her lips once more, then kissed him again, holding so tightly to him that Gavir would have been hard pressed to push her away again. Not that he wanted to—there was a hunger in her, something that Gavir swore he could feel as strongly as his own blood lust. And that he was just as powerless to ignore. He wrapped his arms around her and returned her kiss with equal hunger. He heard her moan, felt it against his mouth. Pain, lust, or some mixture of both? If it was pain, she didn't seem to care. her hands trailing down his skin, her nails leaving narrow furrows of heat behind. He wondered if that was what it felt like for her when he'd switched on the Easel. Primal power, burning into his skin with white-hot need. He slid his hands down her body, cupping her ass and lifting her, letting her wrap her legs around his waist. He backed up until he felt the seat against his legs. He lowered himself down, tearing his mouth from hers and tracing the line of her jaw with his lips. She threw her head back, and Gavir chuckled.

"I've been looking forward to biting your neck," he whispered against her skin, tasting sweat and salt and the deep musk of arousal. He set his teeth against her skin and felt her shudder.

"I want to fuck you, Iras, he whispered against her skin. "I want to hear you screaming my name."

"Like this?" she asked. "I can ride you—"

"That's not what I want," Gavir interrupted. He picked her up and stood, setting her on her feet. "Out of the water." He followed Iras out of the pool, not bothering to dry off as he followed her to the bed. There, he stopped, considering. "Stand at the foot. Don't move." He turned and walked over to the rack, picking up a spreader bar and several long lengths of rope. When he came back, he found Iras standing where he'd ordered her, her wrists crossed behind her back.

"Hands in front," he said. She held her crossed wrists out to him, and he lashed then together quickly, tugging hard on the ends. When he was satisfied, he nodded and let her hands fall. "Spread your legs."

It took a moment to get her in position, with the spreader bar between her ankles, and then tethered to the legs of the bed. When he was done, she could neither open or close her legs, and her balance was a precarious thing. Gavir held her steady, pushing between her shoulders with one hand to force her to bend. He shoved a cushion under her chest, then pulled the long end of the rope binding her wrists to the head of the bed and tied it off there.

"This will do, I think," he said as he walked back behind Iras. "This will do nicely." He ran one hand over her ass, down her thigh and back up, plunging two fingers into her cunt. She gasped, pushing back against his hand. "Well, you're wetter than I thought you'd be. And here I thought I'd need to get you ready for me," Gavir said with a laugh. He pulled his fingers out, then thrust them into her again, watching as she squirmed and moaned. Somehow, he was certain that she'd never beg. Not that he had the patience right now to see if he could push her that far.

He pulled his fingers out once more, trailing damp lines over her hip as he moved to stand behind her, close enough that his cock was nestled snugly against her ass. She whimpered softly and pushed back against him, then yelped when he slapped her ass.

"Impatient girl," he murmured. "You'll get it, don't you worry. I won't leave you hanging." He leaned over her back, running his hands over her sides, finding the points that made her whimper and howl and fight against him and the bonds. He laughed, dragging his nails up Iras' sides, not bothering to avoid the livid red welts that crossed her ribs. The pain made her arch, and the movement of her body made Gavir catch his breath. It was time.

He said nothing, standing and moving back a step, watching as she craned her neck to see where he was. He should have blindfolded her. Too late now. He smiled and stepped forward, his cock in his hand. Iras was hot, wet and open for him, making throaty little gasping sounds as he slowly filled her. Once he started to move, she peaked almost immediately, and he grabbed her hips to keep her from collapsing when her knees buckled. He didn't stop, thrusting harder against her, his fingers digging into her hips hard enough that he knew she'd be able to add matching bruises to the list of marks he'd left as tokens for her to remember tonight. He heard Iras starting to keen again, felt her growing tighter around him as he slammed into her, feeling his own orgasm burning through his blood until he burst, shouting as he came, hearing Iras' cries mingling with his own.

Gasping, blinking sweat out of his eyes, Gavir steadied himself and coughed. "Control! Release the spreader bar."

Affirmative.

Gavir heard the clatter as the bar hit the floor, and he helped Iras up onto the bed, where she collapsed like a cut-string puppet. Gavir grinned, amused, then went to fetch one of his daggers. He sliced the ropes that bound Iras to the bed, and she smiled and curled up on her side.

"Happy?" Gavir asked.

"Floating," she murmured, her voice slurred.

Gavir laughed again, then went back to the plunge to wash. He dried off, and started to get dressed, and by the time that he had put on his boots, the breathing coming from the bed was soft and regular. He walked over and looked down at Iras' sleeping face, at the small smile that graced her lips. He leaned down and kissed her temple; she stirred and sighed softly, but didn't wake.

"I'll see you tomorrow, lovely Iras," Gavir whispered.

Chapter Two

F resh from regen, and with her new skin itching like mad, Iras came out of the lift and started down the corridor to the commissary. Someone called her name, and she turned and smiled to see Marga, one of the Tarken who started service the year after Iras had. Marga had already confided in Iras her own desire to take the Red, and they had bonded over gossip of shared patrons.

"You look good for someone who's been at the end of Gavir's brush," Marga teased as she caught up to Iras. "Hungry?"

"Starved. You know how regen is."

"Yes, I know. Come on. We'll get a bite, and you can tell me about him."

Iras looked at her friend, puzzled. "But, he's had you, hasn't he? What do you want to know?"

"He did, a few months ago." Marga nodded, linking her arm into Iras' and steering her into the commissary. In a corner, she pushed Iras into a chair. "What do you want to eat?"

"Marga, you don't need to coddle me!"

"I'm not! I'm bribing you. I want to hear every little detail." Marga leaned in close. "He had me hard on the Floor, then he didn't sleep with me. I want to know about his cock, woman!"

Iras giggled. "When you put it that way... whatever is ready, and a lot of it. I'm starving. If you make me wait, I'd eat you!"

"Promises, promises," Marga teased. "I'll be back."

Marga was back several minutes later, carrying a heavily-laden tray. She set plates and bowls down in front of Iras, then picked up her own bowl and smiled. "Eat first. Then tell."

Iras laughed, picking up the closest bowl, one filled with a bean-and-grain soup that she usually disliked, but that today tasted better than anything she'd ever eaten. She'd finished the soup quickly and had moved on to devour a roasted vegetable dish when she realized that Marga had set her bowl aside and was watching with wide eyes.

"Are you sure you're all right?" she asked softly. "I've seen you out just of serious regen before, and you never ate like this."

"It wasn't that serious. I mean, yes, there were deep tissue burns. Quite a bit of damage under the skin that I don't think either of us suspected. From the surface, it looked like simple burns, but underneath... Well, I knew it hurt, but until the medics got a look at me——"

Marga shook her head, then lowered her voice, "Iras, do you know how long you were in regen? Didn't they tell you?"

Iras blinked, confused. "Just overnight——"

"Three days."

"What?"

"You were in regen three days. Oh, and he's been here. Every day. For three days. I'm not sure how, but he was in the medical center, by your capsule, every day, for an hour. And you were functional enough for him to want to sleep with you after having you on the Easel? Iras, you frighten me sometimes."

Iras licked her lips and looked around, then leaned forward and softly said, "I was functional enough to throw myself at him when he told me he wasn't going to sleep with me right then and there."

"Iras!"

"Marga, you know how it is!" Iras leaned back, winced slightly at the pressure on her still-tender back, then reached out and picked up a piece of bread. "They treat us like meat, most of the time, regardless of the good that we do for them. For most of them, we're something to hit and something to fuck. He... You've had him. You know."

Marga smiled, a somewhat dreamy expression on her face. "I know. Now that he's had you, though, he won't want the rest of us."

"Don't cast yourself in shadow, Marga." Iras laid her half-eaten piece of bread down and looked at the array of still-full bowls. "I don't know what to eat next."

"Drink, then. You need to drink, for burns. And the tea will help with the pain."

"Right." Iras shook her head and picked up her tea. "I don't know. There's something... different about him. I can't put my finger on it." She took a long sip and sighed. "I also can't wait to see him again."

"Ah, so you're the newest member of the Gavir appreciation society." Marga laughed and tossed her napkin on the table. "You can join the rest of us in mooning over him. I heard about you and his hair, though. That little story made the rounds faster than anything I've heard since I started."

"It was annoying me," Iras admitted. "His hair in his eyes, it makes him look... I don't know. Young."

"He is," Marga said. "He's only twenty-eight." She leaned forward and whispered. "And there's a rumor that he's the Ran-ti-ar's own son."

"Really?" Iras frowned, thinking of Quaran and the few times she'd seen him. The one time she'd had the chance to serve him. She shook her head. "They're nothing alike. Gavir is—"

"Unique?"

"I was going to say special." Iras set aside her empty teacup and picked up another bowl. "So, let me stop talking and start eating. Tell me about your night, Marga. Who had you?"

"Not yet, you don't. You're not putting me off that easy. How is he in bed?"

Iras felt her face grow warm, and was startled by her reaction. "I... he was... very sweet," she said softly. "Not the best lover I've ever had. He seemed... I don't know. Not as brutal as most of the Swords. Not as imaginative, in the bedroom. There are others who know more about technique, but... he was almost..." she paused, thinking. "Reverential?

Yes, I think that's the word. And... Marga, I'd have him again in a heart-beat."

Marga blinked, looked closely at Iras for a minute. Then her eyes widened. "Iras, are you in love?"

"After one night?" Iras laughed, but she could hear how strained it was. "I'm not a silly school-girl, to fall in love after one kiss, no matter how sweet it was."

"You're certainly blushing like a school-girl. And he was here, worrying over you, for three days. I think you may not be the only one."

Iras looked down. "Marga—"

"All right. I'll leave it. But the next time he comes in without an appointment, I'm throwing myself at his feet. Maybe he'll look at me that way... Iras?"

Iras shook her head as she rose, mumbling something about no longer being hungry. She hurried from the commissary, unable to sit still any longer under Marga's too-piercing gaze, or bear the thought of Marga under Gavir's hand. Her own reactions were confusing, and she wanted the solitude of the meditation chambers to think, and try and understand. Perhaps she'd spend the evening with a counselor—

"Iras?"

She turned, her hand hanging in mid-air, caught in the act of reaching for the door controls. One of the newer trainees, a lovely Aakari refugee named Akesha, was coming towards her.

"Iras, there's a Sword looking for you," Akesha said. "He's in the small receiving room."

"A Sword?" Iras knew immediately who it had to be. "Oh. Oh, ah..." She stopped, trying to force her scattered thoughts into some kind of order. "Would you... bring him a drink? And see if he needs anything else? I'll... I need a moment."

"Iras, are you all right?" Akesha asked. "You're flushed. You don't look well."

Iras forced a smile. "I'm still a bit off center from the other night, and from the regen. I'll be fine. Thank you. Very good instincts, Akesha."

Akesha flushed with pleasure, gave the odd half-bow traditional to the Aakari, and hurried away. Iras watched her for a moment, then silently cursed. Not enough time to collect herself. But enough time to, perhaps, mask the fact that she needed collecting in the first place. She hurried back down the corridor towards the living quarters.

———●———

TEN MINUTES LATER, Iras knocked on the archaic swinging door that led into the small receiving room. She heard Gavir's voice from inside:"Come in."

She slipped through the door and saw him standing near one of the overstuffed chairs. He was in his full uniform, armed, and his hair was slicked back. She stopped, closing the door and studying him for a moment. There was an air to him, a formality that hadn't been there when she'd seen him last. That night, she'd seen Gavir. This... this was the Kian-ti-os.

"This isn't a social call," she said finally.

"No, I'm afraid not," he answered. "I wish it were. I promised you dinner, but... I've got to go. There's been an outbreak of fighting in the Gap, and Maryst is threatened."

"Who would threaten the Neutral City?" Iras gasped.

"Desperate people, who won't accept that they lost the war five years ago," Gavir answered. "I'm sorry. I really was looking forward to spending time with you. When you were conscious, that is. I didn't realize how badly I'd hurt you. I'm glad to see you're out of regen. Now... let me see you, before I go?" He made a small motion with his hand. "Turn around."

Iras looked at him oddly, then turned in a circle. When she was facing him again, she could see him nodding. "You're moving well. But your color is off. Are you all right? Truly? They wouldn't tell me much."

She paused, then decided not to try and hide from him. At least, not hide everything. "There was deep tissue damage. Burns under the skin, where they couldn't be seen. I'm fine now—"

"No, you're not," Gavir interrupted. "I can see that, and I'm sorry. As much as I enjoyed hurting you, I didn't mean to hurt you that badly. I've never put someone in regen for three days before, Iras." He stopped, then snorted. "Someone I like, I mean. I am truly sorry. Now, you're off the schedule. For how long?"

"Three more days, with a reevaluation on the third day, just in case."

Gavir nodded. "Well, hopefully, these will keep you busy that long?" He picked up a satchel that had been sitting on the floor next to the chair, and held it out to her. "I wasn't sure what might interest you, so I brought a variety. We can discuss them over dinner when I come back."

Intrigued, Iras opened the bag only to find that it was full of books. She recognized a recent popular novel on top, and under that, a collection of Aakari poetry with a tattered cover.

"Books?" she said, looking at him. "You brought me books? Are they yours?"

"I do know how to read," he answered, his voice oddly tight.

"That wasn't what I meant!" she protested. "I'm sorry, Gavir. I didn't mean to offend. I didn't mean to say I didn't think you could read. It's just that most patrons don't think *we* can read. Apparently, they think that when the Arena isn't open, we lounge around all day, mooning over their swords, sexing each other and eating sweets. Most of the time, if there is a morning gift, it's some kind of... of frippery. Scent is what I usually get."

He looked puzzled. "You weren't wearing scent last night. And you're not now."

"I don't. None of us do, out of respect for the Ishkarin's enhanced sense of smell. If we all wore scent, then the stink on the floor would be unbearable. But no one seems to notice that," Iras said as she sat down on the couch and took another book out of the bag. This one was a treatise on religion in Aakar, and Iras smiled as she flipped it open. "Oh, I have this one."

"You've read it?" Gavir gasped.

Iras looked up, expecting to see disbelief on Gavir's face. Instead, he looked delighted. "I haven't finished it yet," she answered.

"Where did you even find a copy? That one is proscribed! From what I understand, Emperor Tragar had all the copies burned when he named himself a god and overthrew the old Aakari religion. It took me two years to find a complete copy."

"One of the Aakari trainees brought it with him. He told me that his mother was a priestess, before everything. He loaned it to me."

"Will you finish it?" he asked, a note of pleading in his voice. "I've only just read it myself, and I wanted to discuss it with someone. It explains so much of the Aakari mindset, even given that these religions were outlawed years ago. And the parallels between their religion and what was done with the Ishkarin—"

"None of your men will read it?" Iras asked.

Gavir made a face. "Not many of my men read for pleasure. When they do, it's usually popular trash. Not this kind of thing." He came over and sat down next to Iras. "I really can't stay... but I don't want to leave."

She looked at him, found him studying her, and felt her face warm under the intensity of his gaze. "I don't want you to leave, either. Be careful?"

"I'll be careful." He shifted, moving closer, so that his leg was pressed against hers. "Kiss me goodbye, my Iras?"

Iras turned in her seat and reached for him, found his arms closing around her. His mouth met hers, and the delicious hunger that she remembered from the plunge filled her. She wasn't entirely certain if the hunger was hers, his, or if some combination of the two. She also didn't care; she shifted, twisting in his arms until she was straddling his legs, her hips pressing hard against his, feeling the heat of his erection through the synth-leather of his trousers.

He pulled his mouth away from hers and whispered, "Iras, stop. We have to stop. I have to.. to go." She nipped his lip, lightly, but the results were electric; he growled and twisted, pushing her down onto the couch, missing the cushions entirely and tumbling them both onto the floor. Iras yelped as she landed, pain lancing through the not-entirely-healed burns on her back as she hit the floor with Gavir's weight on top of her. Steel clamps closed around her wrists, pinning them to the ground, and it took her a moment to realize that what was holding her was actually Gavir's hands, trapping her arms on either side of her head. He straddled her, his face looming over hers, still growling, a wild light in his eyes. She knew the bloodlust when she saw it, could already feel the heat between her thighs as her body responded. Her hips strained upwards under him, begging silently for the gentle roughness that he'd shown her in the Arena. He smiled, then leaned down and kissed her again, his chest pressing her helplessly into the floor; she moaned against his mouth, a sound that didn't even come close to drowning out the chime that came from Gavir's wrist-comp. He raised his head, snarled, then went still, his eyes closing. For a long moment, he didn't move, and the only sound in the room was his harsh breathing, and the gradually increasing volume of the incessant chime. Then he took in a long breath through his nose, let it out, and rolled off of Iras to sit next to her on the floor. He raised his wrist and touched a button. "Gavir."

"Kian-ti-os, where are you? We're scheduled to lift in twenty-five!"

"I'm on my way, Demarti. Out." Gavir lowered his hand into his lap, took another long breath, then looked at Iras. "Is this where I apologize? I shouldn't be taking such liberties when you're not on duty."

She sat up and shook her head. "Perhaps we should both apologize? I shouldn't have goaded you, knowing that you had to leave. Do you want me to... ah?" She looked down at the prominent bulge in his trousers. "Gavir, I can't let you leave like that!"

"As much as I appreciate the offer, I've got no choice, Iras." Gavir slowly got to his feet and held his hand out for Iras, helping her up. "I'll call on you when I come back. I shouldn't be in the field too long. A few days. A week at the most."

"Be careful," Iras said softly. She moved in close, resting her hands on his chest and rising on her toes to kiss him on the cheek. As she settled back, she noticed for the first time how startlingly green his eyes were. He smiled as she stepped back, looked down at himself, then nodded.

"I'll be back as soon as I can," he said. Then he was gone.

———◉———

SOFT TAPPING. IRAS ignored it, focusing within, seeking the peace that deep mediation could bring. Seeking, and not finding. Again. It had been over a week since she'd been able to find any sort of peace.

More tapping. Then a soft voice, "Iras?"

Iras bit down on the urge to snap, knowing that the display of temper would just feed the flock of rumors that had been swarming through the Dormitory over the past two weeks. All of which came down to the same thing—Iras the untouchable, the Queen of the Arena, was in love.

It wasn't uncommon for the Collared to fall in love with their Patrons. Love affairs were a way to pass the time, and the constant ebb-and-flow of who was romantically partnered with which Sword was a constant source of amusement in the Dormitory. But Iras had never allowed anyone to get that close. Others called her the Ice Queen, and laughed. But she knew the truth. Having someone that close was dangerous. Close meant that someone might learn things she'd rather were kept buried.

How had Gavir, in one night, managed to get so close? And where was he now? A few days, he'd said. A week at the most. It had been two weeks without a word, with no news of the fighting in the Gap, and Iras found herself growing more and more restless, to the point that the counselors had banned her from the Floor. She was too distracted to concentrate, they said, which made her a danger to herself and to any potential partners. So she waited, idle, and tried to meditate.

"Iras?"

"What is it, Marga?" Iras asked, turning towards the door. Marga hovered there, her concern clear, and its very presence grating on Iras' nerves like a tune played ever so slightly off-key.

"You wanted to know if there was news. Demarti Zaan-ti is here."

Demarti? Why was that name familiar...?

"Demarti? He... he serves under Gavir!" Iras bolted to her feet. "He's here? In the Arena?"

"He's taken Raizi, and they've already gone to the Floor. But he was boasting, in the Lounge. They found the rebels and beat them back. Gavir was injured, and he's in regen at the College of Physicians in Maryst." Marga came closer. "He's alive, Iras. And he'll be home soon."

Iras stared at Marga for a moment, wondering where all the air in the room had gone. She swallowed and nodded. "Thank you. For letting me know. I... I might just sleep tonight, knowing."

"You could go to him," Marga suggested. "Take some time. Maryst isn't all that far—"

"No. No, I can't," Iras answered. Too fast, and she could see the odd look that Marga was giving her. The last thing she wanted for for Marga to look too close. To realize that not once in over five years of service had Iras ever left the Arena. So she forced a smile and a laugh. "I can't let him think I'm going to keep throwing myself at him. He's safe, and he'll come to me."

Marga smiled. "Now you're sounding like you. I'll leave you to meditate. Then get some sleep. Maybe tomorrow they'll clear you to go back to service."

"Maybe. Thank you, Marga."

Marga smiled and left, closing the door to the meditation room. Iras sank slowly to the floor, buried her face in her hands, and cried.

⎯⎯⎯◉⎯⎯⎯

THE FOLLOWING DAY, Iras was at last cleared to return to service. Relieved, she went through the rest of the day singing, and that night, she put on the red with exceeding care.

"Do you have an appointment for tonight?" Marga asked, coming to stand next to Iras at the mirror.

"No. They canceled all of my appointments for the next few days when they pulled me. I could stay in tonight, if I really wanted to. But—"

"But you're bored," Marga finished.

"Yes," Iras agreed, smiling at herself in the mirror. "I'm bored. I've read all the books Gavir left with me. He has odd tastes."

"Oh, sounds like someone I know," Marga teased. Iras laughed and poked her, then leaned forward to examine her reflection, brushing a bit of color onto her cheeks. She stood back and looked critically at herself—her color was still off, just a touch. But that wouldn't be looked at amiss. After all, the word that had been spread was that she'd taken ill.

"Are you sure?" Marga asked softly. "Are you ready to go back?"

"I can't hide forever, Marga," Iras answered without thinking. She stopped, frowned slightly as she realized what she'd said, then shook her head. "The Floor is my home. It's where I belong."

"Right." Marga didn't sound convinced. Frankly, Iras didn't think she sounded all that convincing. She forced a smile and turned.

"Shall we?"

⎯⎯⎯◉⎯⎯⎯

AS IRAS WALKED OUT into the Lounge, she heard the conversations closest to the door stutter to a stop, a silence that spread as she moved further into the room. How long had it been since she last walked through those doors and not gone straight into the arms of a patron waiting just for her? She couldn't remember. She heard almost frantic conversation starting behind her, and wondered how many of those voices were querying Central Control, trying to find out if she was free.

"My Lady Red," a silky-smooth voice from behind her said. She turned, and saw a tall male Sword had come up behind her. He bowed slightly. "If you're available, my lady, then I would be honored—"

"She's taken, Demarti."

Iras turned at the familiar voice. "Gavir!"

He smiled as he came up to stand next to her, but she could see that he was moving stiffly, and his pallor was alarming. He rested his hand on the small of her back. "I called ahead to see if you were on. Did you miss that you had an appointment?"

"I did. I knew that my appointments have been canceled, and didn't think to check before I came out. I apologize, Sir." She leaned into him. "I'm glad to see you're well."

"I almost wasn't. Thank you, Demarti. And better luck next time." He dismissed the Zaan-ti with a wave, drawing Iras off to a table in the corner. She sat down, and watched as he lowered himself gingerly into the chair facing her.

"How badly were you hurt?" she asked softly.

"Badly enough, and I don't take regen as well as some I could mention," he answered and grimaced. "Why were your appointments canceled? I heard something about you being ill?"

"I wasn't," Iras answered. She looked around, then reached across the table to touch Gavir's hand. "I was worried. You were gone for so long, and there was no news—"

"You were worried about me?" Gavir asked. "Iras, I'm shocked. And flattered."

Iras looked away, trying to control her embarrassment. "You should be."

"I'm honored," Gavir said. He took Iras' hand in his and squeezed her fingers. "I just wish I were in better shape right now. I'm not in any condition to see to you the way you're needing, Iras."

Iras arched an eyebrow, feeling a surge of indignant anger. "Really? And what do I need, Kian-ti-os?"

He didn't rise. He just smiled, gesturing to one of the gray-clad novices who acted as servitors in the Lounge. He didn't say anything until a pair of drinks had been delivered to the table. Then he leaned forward, and his voice was a low growl when he answered, "You need to be bound. Bound to my whim and paraded on a lead throughout the Arena so that everyone knows you are mine. You need to be beaten, often and thoroughly, so that you never forget just how much regard I have for you and how dear to me you truly are. And you need to be taken, bent over a table and savaged until your screams of pleasure and your cries for mercy ring from the very rafters. That, my dear Iras, is what you need." He sat back, raised his drink, and smiled. "Unfortunately, it's not what I can give you. Not tonight. Would you settle for dinner?"

Iras blinked, and wondered for a moment what had become of her wits. She licked her lips, took a sip of her drink, and said "Dinner?"

"Yes. Dinner." Gavir grinned. "Sorry, I appear to have stolen your brains. Dinner. The meal you eat after midday and before bed. We can leave now, and be back before whatever curfew you might have."

"Leave?" Iras froze. She was still too far from her normal calm, and the very idea of leaving, even on Gavir's arm, sent her into a near panic for the first time in years. "I... I can't leave."

Gavir frowned. "It's not against the rules. I checked. You go get dressed, and I'll meet you down in that receiving room where we met before. I was going to take you to *The Liahn Grove*, but if you have someplace you'd prefer—"

"We can eat here," Iras interrupted. Couldn't leave. Couldn't. If she left, they'd find her...

"Iras, I promised you a night out," Gavir said with a laugh. "We can always eat here. I wanted this to be special... Iras? Iras, you look terrified!"

Iras pushed her glass away, watching as it tipped over and spilled sticky-sweet cordial all over the tabletop. She rose, staggering like a drunkard, her usual grace fled. "I... I have to go. I... I don't feel well."

"Iras, what's wrong?" Gavir stood up, reached for her. For a moment, all she could do was stare, until his hand closed around her upper arm. Panic took over, and she tore free from his grasp and fled.

Chapter Three

Gavir growled, dodged the incoming blow, and charged his opponent. He raised his left hand dagger, knocking aside the sword-blade that had been aimed at his head, and drove his right hand dagger into the attacker's chest. Registering the kill, the training machine whirred to a stop, and Gavir stepped back, panting slightly and wincing at the pull of still-sore muscles in his side.

"Should you be working that hard? I didn't think you were cleared by the medics yet."

Gavir turned, forcing himself not to snarl at Delan. "I'm not. This is all I can do," he answered, his voice tight.

Delan grunted, coming into the salle. "She still won't see you?"

This time, Gavir did snarl. He jammed his twin push-daggers into their sheaths on his thighs, then went to the table along the wall and picked up a towel. He wiped his face and turned to Delan, leaning back against the table. "It's been three weeks. She refuses my appointments, she refuses to see me if I call on her. My notes come back unopened, and just today, I got back a box with the books I lent to her before we went north. Delan, all I did was offer to take her to dinner!"

"Found out something interesting," Delan said. "I chatted last night with one of the White Collars. Sweet girl named Marga. She and Iras are close, she said. Did you know that Iras never leaves the Arena?"

"That's ridiculous," Gavir scoffed. "They all leave. They shop. They go out. All of them. We've seen them."

"Not Iras. After that little episode with you, Marga did some research. She's been worried. The whole of the Arena has been worried about Iras, after that. She's... well, she's like some combination of their mother and their patron goddess in there. The energy in the Arena is off, and it's all because of what happened that night. And no. Iras doesn't leave. From what Marga could find out, Iras hasn't left the Arena since she entered training."

Gavir shook his head. "That's... not right. Why?"

Delan shrugged. "No idea. I've only just gotten off-duty, and I was going to go and find out. Want to come? I was heading to my quarters."

Gavir stood up. "Lead on. I want to know what happened. She was terrified, Delan. And not of me. She was terrified of leaving. Something or someone outside the Arena scares her, and I want to know what."

"So you can kill it?" Delan asked. Gavir didn't answer. He simply smiled.

Delan's quarters were larger than normal for a man of his rank, cluttered with electronics. Gavir looked around, startled at the mess. "This isn't regulation, Delan."

"I'm not, either," Delan answered drily. "Come on, man. You know I'm a Sword by courtesy only. The tinkering that Mathias did to all of us first-gen didn't take with me. Not the way it did with the others. That's why I'm a quartermaster, and not out in the field."

Gavir looked closer at his quartermaster. "I didn't know that. It's not in your files. And I'd wondered. So why do you stay?"

"Because outside of uniform, I'm an old man with no purpose and no caste," Delan answered. "Here, I can be of use. Now come and sit. I'll need you to log in to the terminal for a general search."

Gavir joined Delan in front of a computer system that looked suspiciously more advanced than anything in Gavir's own quarters. "Why do you need me to log in?"

"Because your rank will get us more answers, oh esteemed Kian-ti-os."

"Stuff it, Delan," Gavir growled. Then he grinned. "Voice or keyboard?"

"Voice is fine."

Gavir nodded and addressed the terminal. "Voice print recognition. Gavir Kian-ti-os. General search all areas."

Confirmed.

Gavir looked at Delan and arched his eyebrow. Delan nodded and leaned forward. "Query. Iras Taramar. All records. Hard copy. Go."

The search was over quickly, and the resulting stack of pages was very small. Gavir looked over the printouts and noticed something.

"There's nothing here before she entered training." He looked up at Delan. "These records are linked to her identichip, aren't they?"

"Yes. So how can there be nothing prior to five years ago?" Delan stroked his chin and scowled. "Query. Iras Taramar. Location of birth. Display. Go."

Negative.

"Negative?" Delan repeated. "How can that be negative?"

Gavir shook his head and cleared his throat. "Query. Iras Taramar. Identichip code. Display. Go."

Insufficient authorization.

"Insufficient authorization, my ass. Priority scramble code Razor One Nine Seven. Gavir Kian-ti-os."

Confirmed.

"A priority scramble code?" Delan asked, sounding shocked. "Gavir, you're going to have Quaran on you with both feet if this turns out to be nothing."

"It isn't nothing." Gavir leaned forward and looked at the lines of programming code that spread across the screen. "Delan, look at this. I know you're more technical than I am. I did some work with code in school, but not a lot before I went up north. This—" he tapped the screen. "This doesn't look right."

Delan peered close, frowned. "I do believe you may be right, Gavir," he said slowly. "Is... is it possible to hack an identichip? I've never heard of it happening."

"Anything is possible, Delan. But who, and why?"

"And who is she, really?" Delan added.

Gavir nodded, his eyes narrowed as he thought. Then he cleared his throat. "Query. Date range minus six standard years from tick. Missing persons matching biometrics of Iras Taramar. Hard copy. Go."

Confirmed.

"What are you doing?" Delan asked, watching as sheets of paper spat out of the printer.

"Following a hunch," Gavir admitted. "Iras isn't Aakari. Wrong facial structure, wrong skin tones. She's pure Tyesean. So she should have an identichip implanted at the point where she entered school. Right?"

"Of course. But—"

"Even a no-caste girl would have an identichip," Gavir continued. "So either she came from nowhere, she came from the underground, or she started out as someone else. Which means that someone went missing when Iras walked into the training center." He reached over and picked up the stack of printouts, handed half to Delan.

The two men went through the printouts carefully, and found no signs that any of the young girls who had gone missing in the crazy days after the end of the war had reemerged as the star of the Arena. Gavir tossed the last sheet into the reclamation bin, then scowled at the terminal.

"That was useless," he growled.

"No, I don't think it was." Delan leaned forward. "Query. Date range minus six standard years from tick. Deceased persons matching biometrics of Iras Taramar. Hard copy. Go."

Confirmed.

The stack was considerably larger, and the two men moved to a cluttered table to work, paging through death notices and news reports of criminal investigations. Then Delan stopped. "Oh. Oh, my."

"What?" Gavir got out of his chair and came around to look at the page. When he saw the picture, his jaw dropped. "That's her!"

"Yes, yes it is. Six years younger, and she wore her hair long then. But that smile never changed." Delan scowled. "All right. We know who she is. And who she is... we need to take this to Quaran. But what else do we do about it? Do we do anything?"

Gavir took the page from him and sat back down, studying the picture. He looked up. "Something drove her into hiding. Hiding in plain sight. I want to know what and why. And how I can help her."

Delan nodded, then studied Gavir for a long moment. "You've gone and fallen in love, haven't you?"

Gavir looked startled, then dragged his fingers through his hair. "I don't know, Delan. When I saw her that first time, she was just another female. Now... Now I want to set my teeth into the back of her neck and take her in front of the entire assembled Ishkarin, so that they all know she's mine. I challenged Demarti for her, and he stood down without the fight I wanted. He never even checked to see if I was telling the truth about having called ahead."

"Did you?"

Gavir shook his head. "No, of course not. And the worst part of it? Right now, she won't even see me. That is... Creator, Delan, I've deal with solitary confinement better than I'm dealing with this! All I want to do is find what scared her so badly and destroy it. A lot. Then maybe she'll look at me again. Is that love?"

"Either that, or you should see the medics. Which I happen to know you haven't done. And you should. You're still not recovered from the wounds you took up north." Delan leaned back in his chair. "So, you talked to your father about this?"

"I thought I just did."

Delan's jaw dropped. "*What?*"

Gavir snorted. "I've no idea who he is. Before Felana died, she told me it could have been any one of six. Including you."

"I was friendly with your mother, but not that friendly," Delan protested. "Not that I mind, Gavir. You're a fine boy, and any of us would be proud to claim you."

Gavir blinked, looked away. "Thank you, Delan. Now, what should I do?"

"I'll report this to Quaran. You take *this* to her." Delan held up the death notice. "Tell her what you told me. Tell her you love her, Gavir."

"She won't see me!"

"She will. Show her you have that, and she will."

<hr />

THE SERVANT PEERED into the gloom of the darkened bedroom, fought down the urge to run, then whispered, "Sir?"

"What is it?"

The servant shifted uneasily in place. Disturbing his master after hours was never a good idea. Disturbing him with this news...

"What is it?" The cool voice was just as quiet, but it was as if he'd shouted. The servant jumped, and the printed report in his hands crinkled.

"One of the alerts was triggered, Sir," he stammered. "One... The one you said you would deal with personally."

"Lights. Half power."

The lights came up, still dim, but enough that the servant could see the man rising from the bed. He averted his eyes, hearing his master moving around the room, the rustle of the heavy quilted lounging robe. Then the cough, and he looked up to see his master holding his hand out.

"Give it to me."

Silently, the servant passed the report over, then clasped his hands behind his back, the better to control his shaking. His master looked the page, and frowned slightly.

"This... Have you investigated this query string?"

"No, Sir. You said you wished to handle this alert personally. I brought the report to you as soon as it appeared."

"Good. Very good. Erase all traces of this subroutine, and everything to do with the alert. And forget that you saw this."

"Saw what, Sir?"

The master smiled. "Very good. You're excused." He stepped back into the room and closed the door; the servant sagged in relief on the other side, walking slowly back towards the computer center.

Alone, the master looked at the report and scowled. "Why are the Ishkarin looking into your death, I wonder?" he said out loud. "Computer!"

Acknowledged.

"Query. Iras Taramar. All public records. Display. Go."

Working.

He went to the desk and sat down in front of the terminal, just as information came up on the screen. He scanned through it and looked thoughtful.

"I think perhaps it might be time I explored this Arena abomination," he said out loud. "Perhaps... past time."

———⊙———

THE DOOR SLAMMED OPEN, and Gavir jumped to his feet to see Iras, magnificent in her fury, storming towards him.

"Where did you get this?" she demanded, brandishing the envelope that he'd sent to her when he'd arrived.

"Close the door first," Gavir said. "Right now, there are only two who know this, other than you, and I'd like to keep it that way."

She stopped, her eyes wide, then turned and closed the door; Gavir noted with approval that she locked the door as well. She turned back to him and held up the envelope. "Well?"

"You were terrified of something. I wanted to help," Gavir answered. "I wanted to take whatever it was that made you look so lost and so alone, and rip it into an million pieces. But you wouldn't see me, so I couldn't think of any other way to find out and how in the Creator's name did you change your identichip signal?"

She looked startled at the question. "I... hacked it," she admitted.

"You hacked it." Gavir nodded slowly. "Of course you did. That shouldn't surprise me, knowing who you are. And... may I call you Sirase?"

"No," she said sharply. "That person is dead."

"The identity is dead, but you still live. And you're the Creator's own daughter! You could have come to any of us for help, and we'd have given it, no questions asked."

"Mathias was dead. I was young, and frightened. I'd been kept away from his work, for my own protection, and then because my guardian thought his work obscene. I didn't know I could turn to the Swords for help," Iras answered. "When I had to jump, there was no time to look for other options."

"And why?" Gavir moved towards her, slowly, afraid he was going to spook her into running. "What frightened you? How can I help?"

"Why?" she asked. "Why help me?"

Because I love you, he wanted to say. Wanted to, and couldn't. He sighed and held his hands out. "Do I need a reason?"

"Most people do."

"I'm not most people, Iras. You know me that well, now. Let me help?"

"You can't. No one can. He's powerful, and he gets what he wants. He doesn't know I'm here, and he won't. So I'm safe, so long as I don't leave."

"If that's your wish. Just know that I only want to help you." Gavir said. He held his hand out, his heart in his throat. After a moment, she took it, and he pulled her into his arms, breathing in her scent for the first time in weeks. Just having her that close was like a drug, burning through his veins, and he buried his nose in her hair and just breathed her in.

"I missed you," he murmured.

"I missed you, too," she answered, her arms tightening around him. "And... I'm sorry."

"I should apologize, Iras. I'd no idea." He pulled back slightly and smiled. "Now, I did promise you dinner? How's the commissary here?"

"You want to eat here?" Iras gasped. Then she giggled. "They already think I'm in love with you, you know."

"Do they?" Gavir asked. *And are you?* he added silently. Time for that later. He stepped back and held his hand out. "Shall we go add fuel to the rumor bonfire?"

"Oh, lets!" Iras said with a laugh. She took his hand, letting him lead her out into the hall. Where they were met by a tall man wearing a gold collar, accompanied by an older woman in Council robes. Gavir froze, recognizing both of them in the instant before he put Iras behind him, then wondering at his own reaction.

"Senior Councilor Andradae, Chief Administrator Brinnock," he said cordially. "How may I serve?"

"It's not you we're looking for, Kian-ti-os. We're here to collect Iras Taramar," the Senior Councilor answered. "Or should we say, Sirase a'Mathias."

"Sirase a'Mathias is dead," Iras said firmly.

"You're in remarkably good health for a dead woman, Sirase," Andradae answered. "I'd like to know why. And how. And so would your husband."

Gavir turned, staring at Iras as if he'd never seen her before. "Husband?"

"He is not my husband!" Iras answered, and Gavir could hear the despair in her voice. Then she took a long breath, and drew herself up to her full height. "I deny the marriage contract. My guardian forced it on me, and I refused it. I deny the contract, and I refuse to leave the Arena. I have committed no crime, and cannot be compelled. That is the law."

"As I told you, Councilor," Brinnock murmured.

The Senior Councilor looked sour. "That is the law. But, Lady, your husband—"

"Timaron is not my husband. I deny him," Iras snapped.

Timaron? Gavir's head was reeling. Iras, *his* Iras, was married to one of the worst of the war-profiteers in Tyese? One whose wealth and connections had kept him from being tried for his crimes, even as he drained the resources from dozens of refugee camps. There were rumors of other, darker dealings, but nothing proven. No one had ever been willing to testify against him.

"If that is your final word—"

"It is."

Andradae looked annoyed at being interrupted. "Then the matter will go to the Council. I will see you again, Lady Sirase." She turned and left with the Chief Administrator, and Gavir turned to see Iras looking at him. The anger was back in her eyes.

"This is your fault," she hissed. "Your digging! Now he's found me and—"

"Do you want me to kill him?" Gavir asked quietly. "It would solve the problem."

Iras looked startled. "But—"

"I'd end up in the camps. I know. But I'd do it. For you."

She stared, then her face softened, her eyes filling with tears. She shook her head and whispered. "No. Not for me. Go. Please... just go."

"May I see you again?" Gavir asked.

"I don't think that would be wise."

Chapter Four

For three days, it was quiet. The Council set a barricade around the Arena and declared it closed to all comers until Sirase a'Mathias surrendered into Council custody. The Arena, in turn, refused to allow access to anyone, even Council representatives, declaring that the Council's actions were illegal. Gavir kept constant watch on the stand-off, tried not to worry, and ordered more drills and full-contact combat trainings for the Ishkarin denied their usual outlet. All of Niran City watched with lurid fascination... until the fourth day.

On the fourth day, two ir-Zaans fresh from the training school were involved in a brawl at a tavern near the Warehouse District. By the time the Ran-ti-ar and his squad arrived and put a stop to the fighting, twelve civilians were dead, and twice that injured. Both ir-Zaans were executed on the spot, but the damage had been done. By dawn the next morning, public outcry was overwhelming: The Arena must reopen. Sirase a'Mathias must be taken from the Arena and surrendered to the Council.

Just after midday, Gavir was summoned before the Ran-ti-ar. When he arrived, he was surprised to see that the large room contained not only the Ran-ti-ar, but also the other ranking Ishkarin.

"Gavir, thank you for joining us," Quaran said. He gestured to an empty chair. "I have a question to ask of you."

Gavir sat down, trying to think of a reason why he was being disciplined and failing. "Sir?"

"The woman Iras Taramar. You have had dealings with her. It's well-known. Your feelings for her?"

"Are my own," Gavir answered quickly. "Am I being disciplined, Sir?"

"No. I am asking you to lead the task-force to bring her out of the Arena," Quaran said. "But if your feelings for the girl will in any way impede your performance, I can have Molari take the mission."

Gavir frowned, on the cusp of refusing. Then he lowered his head, thinking hard. Quaran knew who Iras was, assuming Delan had done what he'd set out to do. So he knew what the Ishkarin's duty was to their Creator's daughter. Gavir was also certain that Quaran knew about Gavir's attachment to Iras. So why was the Ran-ti-ar giving Gavir this mission? The man was a good commander, scrupulously fair in his dealings. He wouldn't knowingly torture his second... would he?

Unless... no. Quaran *couldn't* mean.. or could he? Gavir looked up, met Quaran's eyes and saw the answer there. He nodded. "I'll go after her. She won't fight me. She knows what I can do, and... she trusts me."

"Then choose your men. I expect this to be done before sunset. Dismissed."

Gavir rose and bowed slightly, then turned and headed for the door. A soft cough stopped him in his tracks.

"I expect you to report to the medics when you're done, Gavir," Quaran said firmly. "They haven't finished working on you, and it shows in your performance."

Gavir turned back, looked at Quaran and nodded once more. "As you command, Ran-ti-ar." He bowed again, and walked out.

An hour later, Gavir and his team of three other Ishkarin stepped out of an aircar and walked towards the entryway to the Arena. There was one of the Collared at the door, a Aakari-born man that Gavir had enjoyed once or twice.

"Raizi, I need to speak to the Chief Administrator ."

"I'm sorry, Sir. I can't let you in," Raizi answered in his lovely, lilting accent. "We stand by our own."

"I understand that, Raizi. But did you hear what happened?" Gavir waited until Raizi nodded before he continued. "It won't be long, Raizi, before the people demand that we storm the Arena and take her. You know that. And none of you would survive the fighting. It would destroy us all—all of you Collared, and the Swords who depend on you for our sanity. Would she want that?"

Raizi's coppery skin went ashen. He stepped back, then shook his head. "I... I can ask if the Chief Administrator will see you?"

"That's a good boy. Thank you, Raizi." He gestured, and his men fell back several steps, giving the Collared a modicum of privacy.

"We could take him down and get in to get her out. He'd probably thank us."

"Do as you're told, Zaan-ti," Gavir snarled. "We do this peaceably, or you can try your blade on me." Demarti snarled back, but ducked his head when Gavir growled at him. Gavir nodded, cuffing Demarti roughly. "Remember your place, Zaan-ti."

"Sir," Demarti said softly. But Gavir didn't miss the contempt, or the hate-filled glare. There'd be a challenge there, before too long.

"Never you mind, Demarti. Just remember the plan. We can't afford to have any more ill-will from the people, and a riot here wouldn't do us any favors. Or hadn't you noticed we were being watched?" He nodded towards the gates, and the crowd that had formed on the other side.

"Yes, Sir."

Gavir nodded once more and turned back to the entryway, seeing a man wearing a gold collar coming outside. He looked nervous. No, that wasn't right. He looked terrified.

"Chief Administrator Brinnock," Gavir called, walking towards the man. "Thank you."

"Kian-ti-os, you understand that she will not go willingly," Brinnock said without preamble. "I cannot make her go with you."

"For the safety of this city, I have to bring her out. The Council has spoken. If she does not come with us now, then they will allow the Ishkarin to overrun the Arena and take her. I cannot believe that she will allow others to die, Brinnock." Gavir looked back at his men, then faced forward. "Let me speak to her?"

"I... will see if she will see you." Brinnock turned and left without waiting for an answer. Gavir checked over his shoulder to see what his men were doing. Demarti appeared to be regaling the others with some sort of tale, no doubt of his prowess on the Floor. Raizi returned, nodded at Gavir, then looked past him at Demarti.

"That one, he will be trouble," he said softly.

"So I think," Gavir agreed. "Why do you think so, Raizi?"

"He thinks we are only to hurt. That we are not people. When he had me, I was... as an insect to him. Something to be..." he frowned, and Gavir nodded, remembering that Raizi sometimes lost his newly-acquired language when he was feeling strongly.

"Something to be stepped on?" he asked.

Raizi nodded. "Yes, thank you. There is no respect for another life in him. Only the hunter's way. And not even the honorable hunter, like your honored self. He is... as the carrion-eater. Do not turn your back to him."

Gavir looked at Raizi, studying the other man. He'd noticed before that Raizi carried himself with precise control, that his body had muscular definition that Gavir hadn't expected. It had delighted him at the time. Now...

"Raizi, I never asked. What were you, before you came to Tyese?"

Raizi looked startled, then distant. Then he smiled. "In my country, before the end of days, I served in the Imperial Guard. Then the Mad One murdered his honored father, took the throne, and chose to become a God. It was then that I chose to live rather than see my head on a spike outside the palace gates because I smiled when I should have frowned, or because he decided I looked better without. Or because he discovered that I had a fondness for men as well as women."

"The Mad One? You mean Emperor Tragar?" Gavir asked. "I can see why you'd call him that. Anyone who'd slit his daughters' throats, and then take his own life rather than be taken prisoner qualifies as mad."

"The Dark Lords will take him and judge him," Raizi said somberly. "He murdered his wife, as well. The Spider Queen Shajara, because she would not bow to him and call him a god. May they grant his lady and their daughters quiet rest and rebirth, and forgiveness for the sins of their father. And grant that to his son, as well."

Gavir blinked, his attention caught by Raizi's words. "Son? I thought he had only daughters? Five of them, weren't there?"

Raizi frowned, looked away, then looked back. When he spoke, his voice was low, almost a whisper, "There were five daughters. And one son, sworn to the Spider, who refused to bow to Tragar. So he was kept under lock and key, kept away from the rest of the world." He looked puzzled. "You did not know this?"

"No. And I'd wager that the Ran-ti-ar and the Council don't know either, or we'd be combing the refugee camps and the rebel enclaves for him, since we only ever accounted for Tragar and the girls." Gavir ran his fingers through his hair and scowled. Another puzzle. Wonderful. So far as he knew, there had been no knowledge in Tyese of a male Imperial heir. Only the five daughters. There certainly had been no orders given to the troops who stormed the Palace to look for Tragar's son. He made a note to report this to Quaran when he was done, then sighed and looked up. "Thank you, Raizi."

"I serve, Kian-ti-os. And... I trust you," Raizi said. "You... you are in love with our Iras, are you not?"

Gavir was stunned, then let out a sigh. "Am I that obvious, Raizi?"

"As obvious as she." Raizi laughed. "And as unwilling to admit the truth to yourself."

"Raizi!"

"You will take care of her?" Raizi asked. "You will not give her to that man, that... Timaron?"

Gavir met Raizi's eyes and nodded. "I will take care of her, Raizi. With everything I am."

"Then I can ask no more." Raizi relaxed slightly, and Gavir heard the distinctive whine of a stun-blaster powering down. He stepped back, shock overriding the bloodlust, and saw Raizi grin.

"I would not hurt you, Kian-ti-os. Not much. I like you too much for that!"

Gavir started to laugh. "Thank you for that, Raizi!" He turned and shook his head. "You're insane!"

"I wear a Collar. It is much the same thing."

Gavir snorted and raised his voice. "You two, man the gates. When I bring her out, we don't want anyone out there to take a notion to try and liberate the Collared. Demarti, get that aircar hot. When I bring her out, I'll secure her in the back, then you ride guard with her and I'll drive."

Demarti looked indignant. "I can drive an aircar, Sir."

"I've driven with you, Demarti. I'll drive. You guard." Gavir turned back towards the door to wait. He didn't have to wait long—Brinnock appeared in the doorway and brushed past Raizi.

"She will see you, Kian-ti-os," he said quietly.

"Thank you, Chief Administrator." Gavir followed Brinnock inside, grimacing at the palpable tension that marred the normally placid atmosphere that usually filled these halls. Brinnock led him to the lift, then to the small receiving room that Gavir knew so well.

"She's inside," Brinnock said. He hadn't needed to say anything—Gavir could smell Iras' scent in the air. He closed his eyes and fought back the urge to break down the door and drag her down to the Floor. Creator, if *he* was this close to breaking...

He knocked and heard her voice, "Enter."

He opened the door, closed it behind him. She was dressed casually, as if she were a society lady going out for a meal or for shopping. She was sitting in a chair facing the door, and didn't look up when he came in.

"Iras."

"Are you here to drag me out?" she asked softly. "You?"

"No, Iras. I'm here to ask you to come with me."

"I won't."

"If you do not, you know what will happen."

She nodded. "I think so. They'll come in and take me by force. They'll destroy my home and hurt my friends, because a rich, spoiled criminal wants a new toy to break."

Gavir licked his lips and nodded. "That... is about right, yes. Will you let it come to that?"

She looked up at last, and Gavir saw for the first time the shining trails of tears on her face. "No. No, I can't. I just... I didn't think they would send you."

"Iras, I volunteered to come." he paused, then moved in front of her and sank to his knees. Her eyes widened and he saw the hurt in them. "I would not let another Sword do this, not to you. I... I care for you, far too much, to let someone else take this duty. I promise, I will treat you with respect, and I will not allow you to come to any harm."

"You promise?"

"I do. I swear it."

"Then... oh, Gavir, get up!" She laughed, nervously. "It's... you're not supposed to be the one kneeling!"

He arched an eyebrow, and rested his hands on her knees, gently pushing them apart. "I like this position. The view is exquisite." She blinked, then blushed as crimson as her collar. Gavir chuckled, leaning down and kissing the inside of her thigh. Then he rose and held out his hand. "Will you trust me, Iras?"

She looked up at him, hesitated, then took his head. "I trust you, Gavir."

"Then do what I say." He pulled her to her feet, reaching with one hand for the pouch on his belt that contained a set of restraints. She pulled away when she saw them.

"Do we need those?" she asked, her voice strained.

"You're objecting to being tied up?" Gavir found himself fighting back laughter. She looked at him, and must have seen the absurdity; she relaxed and smiled slightly.

"I... I trust you, Gavir." She held out her wrists, and he wrapped the metal bracelets around them and sealed them, binding her wrists in front of her. She shuddered as the second bracelet clicked closed, then looked at him. "Now what?"

"Now, come with me. Listen to what I say, do what I tell you." Gavir put his hand at the small of Iras' back, guiding her towards the door. "And above all, trust me."

She nodded but said nothing. Neither of them spoke on the long walk through the empty halls, down on the lift, or out into the courtyard. As they passed Raizi, the Aakari met Gavir's eyes. He cocked an eyebrow and nodded towards the 'car. Gavir nodded, not quite sure what Raizi was asking. But when Raizi smiled, he knew. Gavir nodded once more and led Iras to the 'car.

"Zaan-ti, stay where you are until I secure her. Then come around and get in on the far side. Understood?"

"Understood, Sir," Demarti answered. Gavir opened the rear door and helped Iras in, securing her belts around her with meticulous care. As he straightened, he noticed the suspicious look on her face. He smiled and mouthed the words "trust me." Then he got out and closed the door.

"All right, Demarti. Other side."

Demarti slid out of the driver's seat and let Gavir take his place, then moved towards the back of the 'car as Gavir closed and locked the door. He had just gotten to the rear of the 'car when Gavir took off, and Gavir heard shouting, heard Demarti cursing as the 'car left the ground. Heard the old insult, hurled like a weapon, and wondered where Demarti had learned *that*.

"Gavir, what are you doing?" Iras shrilled.

"I told you to trust me!" he called back, not looking back. The aircar shook, hard, and he glanced at the screens that showed the rear view, seeing Demarti with his gun raised. He saw the gun buck, and the 'car shook once more, confirming what Gavir suspected. "The bastard fired on us!"

"What?"

"It's all right," Gavir said firmly, glancing at the screen again. At least, he hoped it was all right. Demarti was a damned good shot. He reached out and tapped another screen, starting a diagnostic as he banked the 'car, turning away from Niran City.

"Gavir?" Iras' voice was low, confused.

"Yes?"

"Where are we going?"

"Right now? We're running. Once full dark falls, we're going north to Maryst. You'll be safe there. And once I can set the auto-pilot, I'll let you out."

"But..." her voice faded, and he took a quick look over his shoulder to see that she had her face buried in her hands.

"Are you all right?" he asked. "That bump didn't hurt you, did it?"

It took a long moment before she answered. "I'm fine. But... how much trouble will you be in, Gavir?"

"That's only if they catch me, Iras. Only if they catch me."

Chapter Five

"He called you a freak. A blunted freak. Why?"

It was the first thing either of them had said since Gavir had freed Iras from the restraints. She'd remained in the rear seat, despite his invitation to join him in the front. Gavir didn't turn when Iras spoke, so he was almost certain that she hadn't seen him flinch. "He did?" he answered, trying to sound normal. "I couldn't hear."

"Why would he say that?"

The 'car picked that moment to shudder. The quiet purr of air circulators sputtered and died, and the lights on the control panels blinked out. Gavir reacted, grabbing the controls and tapping the control for the auto-pilot. Nothing happened. He growled and tapped it again, then cursed. "We've lost auto-pilot. Damn it." Gavir looked at the screen and sighed. "We've lost... I think we've lost the main computer."

"Are we going to crash?"

"No, No. I can still control it manually. And the engines are the best shielded part of this craft, so there should be no damage there. But we have no navigation, to start with. I'm going to have to steer by dead reckoning." Gavir looked out the side window at the setting sun. "Thankfully, that's easy right now. We're still heading west. Once we're over the Melnamore, I'll bank and we can follow the river north. I should be able to do that even in the dark."

"If you say so. I can't see much. Gavir, why would he call you a freak? He's a Sword, the same as you."

"You're not going to let that go, are you?" Gavir muttered, low enough that he didn't think Iras could hear. Then he raised his voice, "Iras, I need to pay attention to the terrain and to any pursuit. Without the computer, I don't have scanners."

"All right." She fell silent, and Gavir turned his attention back to the controls. At this speed, and on the course he was taking, they'd reach Maryst... he sighed.

"How are you at math?" he asked.

"Fairly good."

He read her the current speed and altitude, thankful that those gauges were independent of the main computer. "Now, I already told you the route we're taking. About how long will it take us?"

Iras hummed softly for a moment, then clicked her tongue and answered. "About three hours, if I did it right."

"And if you didn't do it right?"

"Then we crash into the other 'car."

"What?" Gavir twisted, looking back over his shoulder, wincing at the sharp pain in his side. Damn it, now not! "What other 'car?"

Iras giggled. "Oh, didn't you ever do that sort of problem at school? One aircar leaves Niran at midday, going so fast, and another leaves Maryst twenty minutes later, going this much faster,. Where do they crash into each other?"

"Really? You do math like that in school? That is... ridiculously morbid," Gavir said. "Why would you want to know where they crash? Wouldn't you want to stop the crash?"

"Don't ask me. I never saw the point."

He looked at the gauges, noticing one in particular was dark. "Damn it. No computer means that I don't know our power levels. I'm not sure we have the power to get to Maryst, and I can't think where we might stop to power up."

"There are ruins all up and down the Melnamore, aren't there?" Iras suggested. "Do you think we could find something there? And I might be able to do something with the computer."

"Given that you hacked your own identichip, I'm sure you could. That's not a bad idea. All right. I'll stop as soon as I find something. Until we get to wherever we're going, are you all right?"

She was quiet for a moment, then murmured, "I'm not complaining. Except that it's lonely back here." There was a lilt in her voice that made Gavir grit his teeth and try not to think too hard about how wide that rear bench really was.

"Don't do that while I'm driving," Gavir growled when he could finally speak again. "Woman, you're not supposed to be getting aroused by being kidnapped."

"It's the company," she answered, and Gavir had to again force himself to pay attention to his driving. "Tell me why?"

"Once we're on the ground." Gavir peered out the windows into the growing darkness, then nodded. "I think I see something. I'm going to land."

⇒◉⇐

THE SOMETHING TURNED out the ruins of what Gavir thought might have been a fishing village. He stopped the aircar in the shadow of a deteriorating wall, then turned around in his seat.

"I've no idea if we're alone here," he said. "Stay with me, or stay locked in the 'car. Understand?"

"I understand," Iras answered. "May I come up there?"

"Please." Gavir turned the passenger seat to let Iras come forward. "If we have to, we can stay here tonight. But I'd rather see you safe in Maryst."

"And what about you?" she asked. "Gavir, what happens to you?"

Gavir shook his head. "Not important. Besides, I'm sort of following orders."

"Sort of?"

"We can't officially help you," Gavir said slowly. "But... you are one of our own, and the Ishkarin protect our own. So... today I was unofficially ordered to help you. Not that I wouldn't have done it regardless! Which, I think, the Ran-ti-ar knew when he gave me the assignment."

"So if we are caught... then what?"

"Then he can deny any official involvement. But I'm not going to get us caught."

"No. No, you're not," Iras said. She looked down at her hands, then took a long breath. "Gavir, take me back."

Gavir stared at her, stunned speechless. Then he found his voice, "Excuse me?"

"Take me back. Because I think I know what's going to happen if we get caught. If they catch us, they'll kill you."

Gavir nodded. "Kill me, or send me to the camps. I know. I accept that."

"I don't!" she cried. "You can't do this You can't... throw your life away! Not for me!"

"Iras—"

"Shut up!"

Gavir blinked and stopped talking, both amused and surprised by her vehemence. When she didn't say anything else, he reached across and took her hands. "May I explain why?"

She looked at him, and nodded without saying a word.

"Iras. My Iras. I've called you that since our first night. Mine. I didn't understand then... but I do now. Iras. I love you. Not seeing you these past few weeks came damn close to driving me insane. Not seeing you ever again? I couldn't do it. Seeing you married to another man? Impossible. I'd kill him first."

"You offered," she said in a small voice.

"I did. And if you told me to right now, I'd find him and rip his head off for you. Cut the top of his skull off and polish it so that you could use it as a soup bowl—"

"That's horrible!"

"Candy dish, then?" Gavir offered. "For people you don't like?"

Iras blinked. Blinked again. Her lips twitched. "You mean like that awful Zaan-ti?"

"Demarti?" Gavir grinned. "Yeah, him, for starters."

Iras shook her head. "You can't. You can't... because then I'd never see you again, either. Gavir, do you know why they took me off the floor?"

Gavir frowned, confused for a moment. Then he nodded. "You mean when I went north. You were sick, weren't you? No... you said you were worried about me. I remember." He realized what she was saying, and felt his world wobble. "You mean... you were sick... but it was because you were worried over me?"

"A few days, you said. A week at the most. Then two weeks went by, and there was no word, and I couldn't find anything out about the fighting or where you were, not without revealing myself. I..." Iras stopped, her hands in Gavir's shaking. "It was when you brought me the books."

"What was?"

"When I fell in love with you." Her voice was quiet, trembling almost as much as her hands. Gavir squeezed her fingers tightly, then gave in to his own need and pulled her across the space between them, pulled her into his arms. She molded herself to him, kissing him hungrily, her fingers working at the catches on his coat. He leaned forward, letting go of her only long enough to help her push the heavy coat off of his shoulders and down his arms, tossing it into the back-seat before pulling her back into a tight embrace.

Mistake. Her hands trailed down his chest to his abdomen, and found the heavy compression bandages that his singlet did nothing to hide. She pulled back and looked down at him. "What... you're hurt?"

"You knew I was hurt, Iras."

"But... that was weeks ago. You were in regen up north—" she stopped, a puzzled look on her face. "You shouldn't have been in regen for two weeks. Especially not at the Physicians College. And you haven't been in combat recently. I know. So this is at least a month old. Gavir—"

"I'm regen resistant," he answered before she could ask. "Always have been. I have to heal naturally. So I hope if we ever have children, they take after you—"

"Don't try to distract me!" Iras interrupted. "How badly were you hurt, Gavir? And how?"

"The how was wrong place, wrong time. A cave fell in on me," Gavir answered. "And how badly... I was lucky. Three of my men died in that cave in."

"Gavir!"

"I was lucky," he repeated. "Broken ribs and a broken head. A concussion. Fairly minor, as these things go. It's the ribs that have kept me off-duty—" he stopped, knowing he'd said too much.

"Off-duty... for three—no, wait. For five weeks. For a month, you've been off-duty. And you haven't been with anyone in the Arena. I'd have known about it—"

"Jealous, my Iras?" The idea amused him far more than it should have.

"I told you not to distract me. How?" she demanded. "How can you go five weeks without release? You should be a—"

"Rampaging monster?" Gavir supplied. "I'm not, Iras. I... I'm different."

Iras frowned, then her eyes widened. "Is that why he called you a freak, Gavir?"

Gavir shook his head, then sighed. He could hear the bitterness in his voice when he answered, "Is that what it's going to take, to prove myself to you? Telling you all my secrets? Yes. That's why he called me a freak. Gavir, the Blunted Freak."

"Blunted?"

"I'm not a real Sword, Iras. I've got no edge." Gavir pushed her back into her chair and dragged his fingers through his hair. "Look, you should work on that computer while we still have the light. I'll lock you in and see if I can find something to charge the packs."

"Gavir?" She reached out and grabbed his arm. "Please, don't leave me."

"We need to charge the packs, Iras."

"Not what I meant. You just pushed me clean out of your world. Don't do that." She reached out and cupped his cheek with her hand. "Gavir. My Gavir. I love you. More than I ever thought possible. You are the most amazing Sword I have ever met. And more important, you are *my* Sword. I don't care what that little idiot called you, except that it hurt you. I don't want you to hurt. Would you explain to me? Please?"

"It should wait, Iras."

"I don't think it can."

Gavir looked at her. Felt the bond between them straining. All or nothing, Gavir. All or nothing.

"I'll tell you mine now. It's short. Then you work on the computer. Once we're in the air again, you tell me yours. Deal?"

Her smile was brilliant. "Deal. But we don't have to wait. I can tell you while I work."

"That won't distract you?"

"I can multi-task. Now, what do you mean, not a real Sword?"

Gavir shrugged. "I'm not. I've been told that... well, I'm a throwback. I was born a Sword, but apparently, I'm not... everything a Sword should be. I feel the bloodlust, and the need, but not to the point of madness. There are some who consider me... deficient. A lot of my trainers. A good number of my cadet group. My mother."

"But you're Kian-ti-os! Shouldn't that prove that you're not?"

"My mother would have told you that it was because I overcompensate. And there are a good number of the Swords who believe that I earned my position because Quaran is my father. Which I don't think he is."

"You don't know?"

"Mother was..." Gavir leaned back and looked up at the ceiling. "Lavish... with her favors. And she never told me who sired me."

"She's dead?"

Gavir nodded. "She died when her squad took the Imperial Palace. I could see the geneticists and find out who my father is, or was. He may very well be dead, too. But there never seemed to be much of a point."

"That makes sense. So, what do you think?" Iras asked.

"About?"

"About why you're the finest Sword alive."

"I'm not." Gavir shook his head. "I'm not."

"You are," Iras insisted. "Or you'd never have made Kian-ti-os. I know how they chose that position, Gavir. It's not popularity. It's skill, and intelligence. You are one of the finest Swords alive, if not the finest, or you'd never wear those rank pins. Everything I've heard about you in the Arena agrees with that. And you agree with that. You don't agree with the others. You... you do agree that you're not what they are, but not that you are deficient. Am I right?"

"I keep forgetting that the Collared are counselors, too," Gavir said. He smiled at her, then tipped his head back and thought for a while. Iras let him, sitting quietly next to him. Finally, Gavir managed to get his thoughts in order. "All right. Yes. You are right. This... I earned my rank *because* I'm blunted. Because I've had to be better, to stay alive. And because I overcompensate. Mother was right about that. I earned my rank because I don't go to the point of madness. I can control myself, more so than some of the first gen. And I work harder, because of it."

"And Demarti and the others?" Iras asked.

"They don't matter. No one else's opinion matters," Gavir answered. He reached out and took Iras' hand. "No one but you."

She smiled and moved back into his arms. "My opinion matters?"

"Yes, my Iras." Gavir reached up and caught the back of her neck in one hand, pulling her face to his and kissing her, hard and fast. Then he let her go. "Now, get to work, love. We can't stay here."

She gaped at him, then burst out laughing. "You're terrible!"

"I thought you loved me."

"I do. But you're still terrible. What do you have for tools?"

"There's a kit under your seat. And the computer access panel is—"

"I know where that is. You go find a generator or something." Iras made shooing motions with her hands, and Gavir laughed, grabbing his coat from the back and putting it on. He checked his gun, then reached back and pulled a box from underneath the rear seat.

"There's another gun in here. And some rations, if you're hungry. I'll be back as soon as I can." He leaned over and kissed her cheek, then got out of the 'car.

<hr />

THE RUINS TOOK LONGER to search than Gavir expected, but yielded an abandoned solar generator. He dragged it out of the wreckage of the storage space where he'd found it and looked up at the rapidly darkening sky. It wasn't too badly damaged, and the panels hadn't been completely buried. Hopefully, it had stored up enough energy to charge the 'car's packs, assuming he could get the thing to work.

By the time he had managed to get the generator back to the car, he was cursing, certain that there was not going to be enough time, nor enough light to go find another option.. He couldn't lift the thing—not with still-healing ribs— so he was forced to drag it all the way. He set the generator up next to the charging port and attached the 'car's charging leads to the generator's terminals before throwing the switch. The generator hesitated for a heart-stopping moment, then an amber light started to glow. Gavir let out the breath he hadn't realized he was holding and left the machine to work, knocking on the side window before opening the 'car's door. And found a gun pointing at him.

"It's me, Iras," he said. "Well done."

"Thank you. I heard you knocking around out there, but I thought if I stayed low, they wouldn't see me." She tucked the gun away, then looked at Gavir. "Why haven't they found us yet? They can track us.

Your identichip. My identichip. The tracking beacon in this car. They should have found us already."

"Good instincts," Gavir said warmly, closing the door. "And I'm willing to bet Quaran is delaying the search. But he can't delay it long. How goes the work on the computer?"

"I've had to do a bit of rewiring. Now I just need to get at the core programming and bypass—"

"You don't have to explain it, love," Gavir said. "I won't understand it. You can teach me later. Now, you have work to do so we can get out of here. And you have a story to tell me."

She smiled and got down on the floor, twisting so that she was laying on her back under the console. "You still want to hear?"

"Yes. Start with the 'chip. How did you hack it?"

"I did it months before I ran," she admitted. "I... I wanted to be useful. My guardian, my mother's sister, she had a fit when I told her I wanted to volunteer in the refugee camps. Said it wasn't fitting for someone of our station. She already hated my father, because he was of a lower caste than my mother. And then he created the Ishkarin, and that was even worse. When Mother died, my aunt refused to come to her funeral, because it meant she'd have to see Father. And when Father died..." She sighed and picked up a small set of pliers. "So I decided to rebel. And it took me... oh, several months to figure out how to get into the chip's programming from the outside. I won't tell you the particulars—it's esoteric, and I'd have to explain quite a bit. When I did, I created Iras..."

Chapter Six

The asylum interview ended as they usually did, with the young Aakari woman weeping in Iras' arms, overwhelmed by both her experiences and by the calm understanding and support offered to her once she reached the Tyesean refugee camps. Iras held the woman close, stroking her hair gently.

"It's all right, Lian. You're safe now. We'll help you," she murmured. "You're amazing, to have come so far on your own. And you're not alone any more. We're going to help."

Lian sniffled and sat up, wiping tears from her face and smiling weakly as Iras offered her a handkerchief. "You're so very kind," she said, her voice shaky. "I don't know how I can repay your kindness."

"There's no need," Iras said gently. "Now, once you're ready, someone will take you down and help you get settled. There are women's dormitories, and a medical facility. I do recommend that you have a medical check—you've been through so much. You'll be given vouchers for clothing, and tomorrow you can talk to vocational trainers, see where you might want to go from here. There's no rush. You can stay in the dormitories as long as you like."

Lian nodded, twisting the handkerchief between her hands. "And then?"

"Well, you have choices afterward. You can stay in Tyese, either here in Niran, or in one of the smaller towns. Vocational training will help you get settled with work, and we'll see you placed in an apartment if you stay in the city If you want to farm, you have that option—there is plenty of arable land in the Highlands, and the Council has provided for a stipend for refugees who want to start farming." Iras looked at Lian and smiled. "If you want to marry, I've no doubt you'll find someone, either here in the refugee camps or once you're out on your own."

Lian blushed. "I hadn't thought that far ahead."

"Like I said, there is no rush. You've your whole life ahead of you now, Lian. Take it one day at a time. There is so much for you to learn, for all of us to learn, now that the fighting is over."

They chatted for a few minutes, then one of the attendants came and escorted Lian out of Iras' little office. Once she was gone, Iras leaned back in her chair and reached for her cup of tea, only to discover that it was cold.

"That took you some time, Iras."

Iras looked up at the sound of the name she used here, and smiled at her supervisor, who was standing in the doorway. Jacari was a handsome older man, with kind blue eyes and an air of lingering sadness to him. People seemed to like him on sight, which was why he was so good at his work in the camps. "She was scared, Jacari. Scared of everything and everyone. It took a while to get her to see that I wasn't going to hurt her. She went through horrors to get here. I don't think I got everything out of her, but it was enough to make me not want to sleep tonight."

Jacari nodded, coming inside and setting a fresh cup of tea on Iras's desk. "Have you seen this?" she asked, setting a datapad on the desk next to the teacup.

"I've seen nothing all afternoon," Iras answered, picking up the pad and looking at the announcement. She read through it twice, then looked at Jacari. "This is serious?"

Jacari nodded. "Combination counselors, prostitutes and pells. The Council wants people to volunteer, and they're remaking the sports arena at the university over for the main facility. There will be trainers here in the vocational areas starting tomorrow."

"They won't get many refugees," Iras mused, picking up the fresh cup of tea and taking a sip. "They've already seen too much, been through too much."

"For high-caste status, there will be volunteers," Jacari said. "I might go down for evaluation." She looked at Iras, then continued. "I think you should, too, Iras."

"Me?" Iras squeaked.

"I think you might be the kind of person that they're looking for. Your empathy ratings are off the charts. You're halfway to being a full therapist, and you're not even legal age yet. Think about it—the term is five years, and you'll get a higher caste out of it in the end. Why not you?"

Iras shook her head. "Because... I can't. I can't explain. I just—" A soft chime rang, and Iras jumped and grabbed at her chronometer. "Is that the time? Oh, Jacari, I didn't realize it was so late!"

"You have to go?"

"I've got an appointment. And I'll never get there in time if I don't dash now." Iras jumped up, shoving the chronometer into the pocket of her coverall. She called a quick goodbye to Jacari, then rushed from the offices and out into the refugee camp. A rather battered looking aircar was parked just outside the boundaries of the camp, along with several other vehicles in various states of disrepair.

"The shopping district!" she snapped as she closed the doors. There was a hiss as the doors sealed, then the 'car lifted and banked. Iras checked the control panels, which were oddly more advanced than should have been found in a car this old and decrepit, then slipped into the rear of the 'car and stripped off the coverall, bundling it up and stuffing it into a bag that she locked in the cargo compartment. She dressed quickly in a fine gown and over-vest that she took from another bag, brushing out her long hair before she slipped back into the driver's seat and opened a small box that proved to contain an assortment of cosmetics.

"Control, how many messages?" she asked as she set about transforming shy, unassuming, low-caste Iras back into Sirase, high-caste daughter of wealth and privilege.

Sixteen calls. Six messages.

"And all from Aunt Destia, I assume?" Sirase asked, looking in the mirror. Good enough. "Play the last message," she ordered.

Immediately, her aunt and guardian's voice filled the cabin. "Darling, I've been trying to reach you for simply ages. We're having a dinner guest tonight. A very influential member of society. Do try to be on time?"

Sirase frowned. "A dinner guest? And she wants me there? That's unusual." Usually, her Aunt preferred that Sirase be elsewhere on the nights she entertained. According to her aunt, it was bad enough that Sirase was the daughter of the man who created "*those Ishkarin monsters.*" She was also "*too intelligent for a girl,*" "*too vocal for a young lady of her caste,*" "*far too conscious of things that she shouldn't even know about,*" a comment that Sirase interpreted as her knowledge of the plight of low caste and no-caste members of society. She was also "*far too perceptive.*" Her conversations made people uncomfortable.

Which meant that there was only one reason they were having a dinner guest tonight, and Sirase groaned as the aircar final approach alarm sounded. A few minutes later, the 'car grounded with a lurch and a long hiss, settling in a space surrounded by several other, more expensive-looking aircars. Sirase powered down the 'car, then got out and walked away, heading down the line of aircars until she reached one that was considerably nicer than the one she'd left behind. It chirped as she approached, and the doors opened.

"Home," she ordered as she sealed the door. The aircar rose smoothly, and Sirase opened a hidden compartment and picked up a small device that she held it against her shoulder for a moment, until it beeped. Hacking into her identichip had been much harder than she'd expected, but it needed to be done— it would never do to have her painfully status-conscious guardian find out just what her wayward charge was really doing with her time. Hence, the creation of Iras. Sirase replaced the device and took out a small transmitter, turning it off. She returned the device to the compartment and locked it, and only then did she lean back and sigh. If her aunt ever had the aircar traced, she would see that it had been parked here all afternoon, and the transmitter had been broadcasting a signal that was a duplicate of the one that should have been transmitting from Sirase's identichip. That and the packages in the cargo space both would lend credence to Sirase's excuse of an all-day shopping trip.

As the aircar entered the traffic stream, the com signal chimed. Sirase touched the stud. "Sirase."

"There you are!" Her aunt sounded positively irate. "Why haven't you answered my calls? Where is your com-link?"

"I told you, Aunt. It ruins the lines of this dress." *And gives you another way of tracking me*, Sirase added silently. "I did get your message, though," she added. "I'll be home in ten minutes at this speed."

"Good. You'll have time to change. I expect you to be polite and pleasant tonight, Sirase."

Sirase rolled her eyes, but kept her voice level. "Of course, Aunt. Who is the mystery guest?"

"You'll find out in an hour." There was a slight hum as the com-signal was severed, and Sirase sighed and rubbed the tip of her nose with one finger.

An hour. No warning, no hints of identity, and her aunt was being coy? That confirmed Sirase's suspicions—another potential suitor. Just how she wanted to spend her evening.

<hr />

THREE HOURS LATER, Sirase was fighting to keep herself from saying something that would alienate her from yet another layer of society. Not that she cared; she already had as little to do as she could possibly manage with the bubble-headed so-called peers with whom her aunt insisted that she socialize. However, she most definitely did not want to spend the next several weeks listening to her aunt bemoaning the fact that she would never be able to show her face in public again, and how could Sirase *do* this to her?

The guest had turned out to be someone that Sirase knew. By reputation only, though, and that was enough for her. His name was Timaron, although among the refugee camp administrators, his name was usually prefaced with the words "That old, officious, incompetent idiot—." If the words were even that polite. There were suspicions that he had been a war profiteer, and he most certainly was profiting from his position as Chief Administrator to the refugee camps. The constant lack of supplies and the poor quality of what they did received showed that a large portion of the somewhat lavish stipend that the Council had allotted to the refugee camps was being diverted elsewhere. There were other rumors, too. Lurid ones, involving Timaron's four marriages, each to a wealthy heiress. Each of whom died after only a few months of marriage.

Meeting Timaron, Sirase could well believe that he was lining his own pockets. He dressed far too well for his caste, and his jewelry was too ostentatious for any caste that included a modicum of taste. Sirase studied him closer under the guise of refilling his wine goblet. No. No, something was amiss. His too-expensive clothing was also two or three seasons out of date, and showed signs of wear and well-tailored repairs. The fancy jewelry was all paste—Sirase could see the gilt chipping from his pendant. And his cosmetics were cheap and waxy, and smelled stale. Sirase returned to her seat and sipped her tea, looking at him, then looking away. When he thought she wasn't watching, he stared at her openly, and there was an oiliness to his gaze that made her uncomfortable.

"This has been a delightful evening, Destia," Timaron said, brushing invisible crumbs from his hands. "Quite delightful. Shall we move on to business now? When will we sign the contracts?"

"Contract?" Sirase sat up straight, looking first at Timaron, then at her aunt. Had she guessed wrong? "Aunt, are you marrying again?"

Destia looked sour and glared at Timaron. Then she smiled at Sirase, a smile that was every bit as false as Timaron's gilt. "No, my dear. Timaron is interested in your hand—"

"No."

Destia looked startled at Sirase's flat interruption. "Sirase!"

"No, Aunt. I am not going to marry someone old enough to be *your* father. Nor am I marrying anyone who profits on the misery of others." Sirase rose. bowed slightly to her aunt. "I'll leave you to your guest—"

"Sit down, Sirase!" Destia snapped. "You are not yet of legal age; you have no say. I decide who you will wed."

"I still say no," Sirase answered, folding her arms over her chest. "Any contract that I sign now will not be binding, nor will I consent to signing a contract once I am of legal age."

Timaron rose, smiling slightly. Others might have thought the expression made him look jovial, but Sirase just shuddered. "Sirase, my dear," he said. "Your guardian has simply... solicited my help in finding you a purpose—"

"My purpose is none of your concern!" Sirase spat. "And stop looking at me like that." She turned away, fighting back nausea. She knew what the oiliness was now: lust. Timaron's lust was getting stronger, strong enough that she could almost hear his thoughts.

"Destia, may I speak with Sirase?" Timaron asked. "Alone?"

"Of course. See if you can make her see sense," Destia rose and swept from the room, the door sealing behind her.

"No, my dear," Timaron said, turning back to Sirase. "There are advantages to being married to me."

"How strange," Sirase murmured. "I can't think of a single one."

Timaron paused, and Sirase felt his confusion before it was again blotted out by desire. "I am a candidate for the Council in the next session. And I am Chief Administrator to the refugee camps. I am very powerful."

"You'll never sit on the Council. And you're stealing from the refugee camps. It's only a matter of time before you're caught." Sirase turned and looked at Timaron. "You have no power. And no money. You want me for mine."

"Sirase, how petty do you think I am?" Timaron chided gently, as if she were a child. "You are a lovely young woman, and I am... a lonely man. Is it any wonder I'm interested in marriage?"

"Why me?" Sirase asked, confused. There was an undercurrent to his emotions now. Something she didn't like but couldn't identify. "If you're lonely, there are wealthy women closer in age to you. Why... oh."

"Children, Sirase," Timaron confirmed. "I've no heir."

Sirase nodded, looking away again. Children. The other stories. His other wives. They all died in childbirth, and Timaron inherited their fortunes.

"I don't want you," Sirase said firmly. "And you cannot force me to sign a contract."

"You are so very naive," Timaron said softly, coming up behind Sirase. He didn't touch her, something for which she was very glad. "Your consent is not necessary, Sirase. Not when your guardian has already given her consent. According to the old laws, you can be married if your guardian wills it so. Your aunt has already arranged it. You will be my wife. She's been searching for a husband for you for months, my dear, and is relieved to be rid of you and your eccentricities."

Sirase turned, staring at him, knowing that he was telling the truth, and yet unable to believe that her aunt would do this. "The contract will not be valid," she whispered. "Not if I don't sign it—"

"A trifle. Your aunt can sign for now as your guardian," Timaron scoffed, dismissing the objection with a wave of one hand. "And you can sign again once you're of age. And if anyone objects... well, money and power exist to change the rules. Come now, will it truly be so bad? One child, one heir to our combined fortunes, then you may do as you like." He smiled, a smile that faded as he reached for Sirase and she evaded his touch.

"When?" she asked, wrapping her arms around herself, trying to control her shivering.

"Our wedding will be celebrated in ten days, once you have reached your majority," Timaron answered. "However, we will sign the contract and formalize our union tonight."

Sirase swallowed around the lump in her throat and shook her head. "Tomorrow," she whispered. "Please. Give me the night to... to absorb all this."

Timaron smiled broadly, obviously thinking that he'd won. "Tomorrow, then."

The rest of the evening passed as a blur. Destia looked more than pleased, and started making plans for an elaborate wedding, but her twittering passed over Sirase, and she remembered none of it when at last she could finally escape to the refuge of her own room. There, she sat at her dressing table and stared at her own reflection.

Tomorrow. Tomorrow, they would sign a marriage contract. Tomorrow, they'd be married.

Tomorrow would start the countdown to her own death. Sirase was certain of it. Absently, she started to rub her shoulder, feeling the ridge underneath the skin that marked her identichip. Her good work in the camps was over, her training all for naught... Sirase frowned, her finger resting right on her 'chip, as a new thought occurred to her

She could become Iras. Cast off Sirase the same way she cast off her expensive clothes when she went to her work, and become Iras truly. But they'd look for her, find her.

Unless... Sirase moved to the bed and lay down, staring at the relaxation mandala on the ceiling as she thought. Yes.... yes... that might work. She'd have to make sure no one was hurt. But it would work. She smiled slightly, running a lock of hair through her fingers. She'd have to be careful. If she rushed, her aunt would become suspicious. If she gave any sign that she was going to bolt, she had no doubt that Destia would keep her from leaving at all. Rolling on to her side, she checked the chronometer. It wasn't too late, but she'd have to move if she wanted this to work.

Quietly, she got up and started to get dressed, pulling on a more practical outfit—trousers, low boots, and a long jacket. She pulled her hair back into a long tail, then sat down on the floor and reached underneath her bed for the most obvious of her hiding places. Yes, Destia had been in this one, Sirase noted with a shake of her head. The generic credit vouchers that Sirase had stashed there were gone.

Sirase rolled to her feet and went into her closet, standing on tiptoe to reach the back of the highest shelf. Her fingers found the cord she was seeking, and she tugged the false shelf back free and took out the pouch where she hid her wages from working at the camps. She tucked the pouch into her inner pocket, then laid the shelf back flat. By the time anyone thought to search her closets, it would be too late. She grabbed an armload of gowns and carried them out into the bedroom, tossing them around carelessly, then sighing, making sure that the sound was both overly dramatic and very loud. A moment later, just as she expected, there was a tapping at her door.

"Sirase?" Destia came inside and looked around, startled. "My, what happened here?"

"I'm going shopping, Aunt," Sirase announced. "If I'm to be married tomorrow, then I have to have something to wear. These... nothing here will do!"

Destia smiled. "Of course, my dear! Wait, I'll come with you."

Sirase fought to keep her face expressionless. How could she not have expected that? "You have so much to do already, Aunt. I'll hardly be any time at all—I saw something perfect in the shops today. I should have bought it then. But I didn't think I'd have any place to wear it before the season changed."

"If you saw it, then you should hurry and go get it before someone else carries it off," Destia said. "Take my credit chip, Sirase."

"Aunt?"

"This will be my gift to you. Go along. And find something pretty to wear with it." Destia smiled. "I know you've never been one for jewelry, but you should have some sparkle on your wedding day. Now go, before the shops close!"

Ten minutes later, Sirase was in her aircar, heading towards the shopping district. She bit her lip to keep from laughing, knowing it was too soon to celebrate her escape. There were still so many things that could go wrong. But if this went right....

Her 'car grounded in the mostly empty parking structure, and she looked around and nodded. The only other aircar in this section was the battered one that she'd left there earlier, when she'd left Iras behind. She knew that there were no cameras in this part of the structure—that was why she parked here. Quickly, she unlocked the compartment and took out her two creations, turning on the transmitter. Then, she took a deep breath, pressed the other device to her shoulder, and waited for the beep. It sounded oddly loud in the silence of the aircar, enough that Sirase—*Iras!*—startled at the sound. She looked at the machine, then locked it back into the compartment. She'd never need it again.

Quickly, she went to the other aircar, letting herself in, changing her clothes and wiping the cosmetics from her face. Iras never wore cosmetics. She looked at herself in the mirror, frowned slightly, then sighed. She should have brought something to cut her hair, something Iras was always saying she would do. No matter. She bundled up her fine clothes and tossed them into the back of Sirase's 'car, then set the controls to head west, toward the ruins of Amali City. The battery packs should get the 'car to Amali before they died and the 'car crashed. It would appear to the authorities that she had been running, that the 'car had crashed. That Sirase was dead.

Iras set the controls and got out, stepping back and watching as the aircar rose, banked, and headed west. When it finally disappeared into the darkness, Iras went to her own 'car and got in, closing the door and taking off towards the refugee camp.

Chapter Seven

"I stayed in the camps for the next ten days. On my birthday, I signed the contract for the Arena and never looked back," Iras finished. She was sitting once more in the passenger seat, her features illuminated by the lights from the now-functional computer screens. Gavir looked at one and noted that the battery packs were almost fully charged. Good enough.

"You are amazing," he said quietly. "To have done all that, all on your own. Now, let's not waste it. The packs are charged enough. I'll unhook the generator and we'll get out of here. Program that thing for Maryst, will you?"

"I've already done that."

"And you're efficient, too. Everything I want in a wife—"

Iras looked startled. "What?"

"Just a moment." Gavir slipped out of the car and unhooked the cables, retracting them into the charging port and sealing it. When he got back into the car, Iras was staring, her eyes wide as saucers.

"Did you... just propose marriage?" she asked slowly. "You said something before about children, but... wife? You want me for your wife?"

"I did just propose marriage, yes. It wasn't all that romantic, but I haven't had the time to shop for a pledge bracelet." Gavir smiled at her. "Sirase Iras a'Mathias Taramar, will you marry me?"

Iras opened her mouth, closed it again, then jerked as an alarm started to sound. Gavir spun in his seat, scanning the controls. "Proximity detectors. Blast it all, they found us. Strap in, love. We're getting out of here." He pulled his own straps on, buckling them as he started the 'car

"I'm in. And yes."

Gavir looked at her, grinned, and nodded. "Good girl. Hold on tight."

He had to drive the 'car out of their shelter in order to lift, and hoped that there was no one yet in the ruins who would see them. If he set the cloaking shield before he lifted, and lifted without running lights, he might be able to make some distance before whoever had found them landed. Assuming they weren't using night-vision, and that whoever was manning the scanners was blind. That thought was dashed when he heard the sharp report of gunfire. His wrist-comp crackled to life, making him arch an eyebrow. Who besides Quaran had the override codes?

"Gavir, you are hereby ordered to stand down and hand over the woman!"

"Oh, Demarti," Gavir groaned. "Who exactly did you fuck to get those codes?"

"What codes?" Iras asked.

"The override codes on this." Gavir held up his wrist. To his surprise, Iras grabbed his arm and unstrapped the wrist-comp, turning it over and opening the tiny control panel.

"Shouldn't you be driving?" she asked without looking up.

"Yes, ma'am. Brace yourself." Gavir pushed the accelerator and pulled back on the controls, taking the 'car into a punishing, near-vertical climb that made the sensors scream as if they were in agony. He held it, one eye on the altimeter and the gravimeter, until he was no longer certain that the 'car could take the stresses. Only then did he bank hard and level off. The alarms went silent, and he took a moment to look at Iras. "Are you all right?"

It took her a moment to answer. Then she nodded. "Yes. Yes, I think so. Could we not do that again?"

"I'll try not to." Gavir pushed the aircar into a cloud bank, then changed direction and increased his speed. The computers seemed to be working now, and he checked the reading before looking at Iras.

And at the now-silent wrist-comp in her hands. "What did you do with the comp?"

"Turned it off."

"You *what?*" Gavir stared in shock. "You... those things don't have an off switch. I know. I've wanted one for years."

"Well, I didn't so much as turn it off as I made it go crazy."

Gavir snorted, checking the proximity sensors again. No pursuit. That was either very good, or very, very bad. "You're going to make me go crazy. Explain."

"I told it to calculate the second to last digit in the Eternal Constant."

Gavir frowned. "That's... that's the one that doesn't end, right?"

"Yes." Iras sounded very smug. "Until I cancel the program, they can't use this to contact you or to track you."

"Clever girl," Gavir said. "I'd tell you to do that to the tracking beacon in the car, but you can't reach it from here and I am not landing any time soon. Toss the comp into the back and take over navigation. I think we may need a new plan. They're not chasing us."

"They're not?" Iras sounded confused. "Why is that bad... oh. They're not chasing us because they don't need to chase us."

"Because we're running straight to them. Yeah, that's what I'm worried about." Gavir looked down. "The most logical places for them to ambush us would be either at the headwaters of the Melnamore, or at the Tyesean mouth of the Gap. So, we have to go another way. Ah... compute a course that will take us into Aakar, and into the Aakari mouth of the Gap. If I'm right, they'll expect us to go any way but that one, since that was where the fighting was. And since there are still rebel enclaves in those mountains, they can't set up an ambush without being ambushed themselves."

"Will it be safe for us?" Iras asked, her fingers already dancing over the nav keyboard.

"Safer than having Swords not in the know firing on us." Gavir looked once more at the proximity sensors and frowned. Had he understood Quaran wrong? Had he read too much into his orders? Was he wrong?

No. Whatever happened, saving Iras had been the right thing to do. So had asking her to marry him. Now, he just hoped they would live long enough to have a wedding night.

———●———

THE COURSE THAT IRAS set took them far out over the Aakari plains, then back in the shadow of the great northern forests. It was full dark before Gavir turned the car back to the east. Iras had fallen asleep, and that left him alone with his thoughts. And his worries. The more he thought about it, the more he was certain that they were being herded. There was an ambush waiting for them—if not at the mouth of the Gap, then at Maryst itself. The city might be neutral, but the ground outside was not. He took a long breath, then let it out and shook his head. Maybe... he reached out and touched the communicator stud. "Direct link. Quaran Ran-ti-ar. Priority scramble code Razor One Nine Seven. Gavir Kian-ti-os. Go."

There was a hiss of static, then a snide voice answered, "Well, hello, Kian-ti-os. Fancy hearing from you—"

Gavir cursed and slammed his hand onto the stud, cutting off Demarti's voice. Things had just officially gone from bad to fuck-all. If Demarti was monitoring the priority scramble channels, that either meant that he had subverted the Ran-ti-ar's authority, or it meant that the Ran-ti-ar had been forced to denounce Gavir. Whichever it really was didn't matter. Gavir's clearances were gone, as was his authority. For a moment, he considered turning the 'car back around and heading west. If they kept going, they could get lost in the Aakari wilds. Maybe make their way to the sea, and the world beyond... but no. He knew full well what happened to Swords who went rogue, who fled into the mountains or into Aakar. He had been part of the hunting parties charged with bringing the rogues back, or else bringing back their heads and their identichips.

Beside him, Iras stirred in her sleep. He glanced over at her, reaching out and brushing her cheek with the back of his fingers. She sighed, but didn't wake. Gavir watched her for a moment, then turned back to the controls. He could survive in the wild, for a time. A year, perhaps two, before they found him. But he couldn't ask that of her. They had to get to Maryst. If he could just get her inside the walls...

By the time he heard Iras' breathing quicken and knew that she was awake, he'd come up with a plan. She'd never agree to it, but he had no intention of telling her the entire plan. Just her part.

"You awake?"

"Yes. Do you want me to drive, so you can sleep?"

Gavir shook his head. "Thanks. But no. We'll be there... maybe an hour? Faster if I push it."

"And they'll be waiting for us there," Iras said. "So, tell me what the incredibly brave, incredibly stupid plan is that you've come up with, so that I can shoot you now."

Gavir turned and stared at her. "What?"

"You're going to throw your life away, so that I can get into Maryst. Don't try and tell me I'm wrong. It's just the sort of terribly honorable and loving sacrifice I'd expect from you. And I will tell you now that if you even try it, I'll kill you myself. And then turn the gun on myself."

"Iras!"

"Then don't even think about making me live the rest of my life with your death driving stakes into my heart!" she snapped back. So much fear in her voice.

Gavir licked his lips, then reached across and took her hand. "You're right. You're right, and I'm sorry. I didn't think of that. Do you have a plan?"

"No. Other than we both go in, or we both die."

"That sounds like more than I had. All right. We both go in, or we both die. I love you, Iras."

"I love you, too. Can you land?"

"What, now?" Gavir looked at the sensors. "Yes. Why? I mean, we do have a portable pot underneath the rear seat. It's not pleasant—"

"That's not what I wanted," Iras interrupted. She paused, and Gavir realized what she was asking.

"Oh. You... I... I see. Now?"

"If we're going to die, I want a wedding night." Iras squeezed his hand. "Darling, I didn't think you would be shy about it."

"I'm not!" Gavir blurted. "I just... I didn't think you would want to. Not until we were safe."

"Are we ever going to be safe, Gavir?" Iras asked quietly. Gavir considered the question for a long moment, then nodded and set the controls to land. Once they were on the ground, he switched off the 'car's systems and listened to the heat ticking off the metal in the engines.

"Iras, I don't have anything—" he started to say as he turned towards her, and caught her as she clambered into his lap, her mouth finding his and cutting off his words. She kissed him with a fervor he hadn't felt from her before, and it took him a moment before he realized what it was.

Desperation. That he could understand, and he kissed her back with heat. There should have been more than just this one night. Should have been, and they both knew that there never would be. Just this one night to make up for all the tomorrows they would never have. It would have to do.

He pulled away from her mouth long enough to gasp, "Back seat." He pushed her off his legs, but she refused to relinquish his mouth, tugging at his coat as they both stumbled over the seats and into the only-slightly more spacious rear seat. There, they tugged and tore at each other's clothes, scattering them over the floor and the bench, until at last they were both bare. Iras pushed Gavir down onto his back, straddling his hips and catching her hands in his own. She pushed them down, pinning them on either side of his head and smiling down at him.

"I've got you," she declared, her voice husky. "You're mine now."

"I always was yours," Gavir said. It didn't seem to matter that he was the predator, and she the prey. He'd fight for her, kill for her. Die for her. And kneel for her, if that was her wish. The roles were reversed, and he knew that it was right. She raised herself up, and slowly lowered herself over his cock, her cunt brushing against the head lightly enough that he gasped and thrust his hips up. The movement sent shooting pains through his ribs, and he gasped.

"No. No, you're not allowed to hurt yourself," Iras chided him gently. "You're not allowed to move."

"Yes, Iras." His voice sounded oddly meek to his ears, and apparently to hers, too—he saw the surprise on her face. Then she smiled and leaned down, nibbling lightly at his lip before kissing him slowly. When she rose, she let go of one of his hands, reaching down and guiding his cock into position, slowly taking him inside of her until her hips were sealed tightly against his. She didn't move for a moment, and Gavir bit the inside of his mouth until he tasted blood, fighting the urge to move, to roll her onto her back and claim her. But the claiming tonight was not for him to do, as Iras slowly started to move over him, around him, her breathing growing faster, more ragged. She let go of his hand, bracing herself with one hand on the rear bench, the other resting lightly on his stomach as she rode him, her head thrown back to reveal her throat. Gavir groaned, reaching out and running his hands down her thighs, catching her behind her knees and holding on as she peaked, gasping and moaning before she fell still. Gavir rubbed his hands up and down her legs, waiting until her breathing slowed before asking, "My turn?"

She looked startled. "You... oh, Gavir. I'm sorry."

"Don't be. That was wonderful to watch." He sat up slowly, wincing a little and not bothering to hide it, then pulled Iras into his arms. "You, lady-mine, are magnificent."

She blushed, then wrapped her arms around his neck and clung to him. "Gavir, I don't want—"

"I know," he answered. "I know. Neither do I."

"Could we run?"

Gavir shook his head, his cheek brushing against Iras' short hair. "They'd come after me. A rogue Sword? They'd hunt me down."

"Then there's no choice." Iras hugged him harder, then pulled back. "Your turn, Gavir. I... I don't think we have anything you can use on me—"

"You know, sex with me doesn't have to be bondage and pain," Gavir interrupted. "Unless you want it that way."

Iras looked thoughtful. "I've never had sex with a Sword that was any other way."

Gavir grinned and tapped her nose with one finger. "That's because your main purpose isn't sex, my dear. It's release. And honestly, I can do more to you with my hands than I could with anything I might find lying around at the Arena. If we had time—"

"Show me."

"Iras, we're running for our lives!" Gavir gasped, laughing. "We don't have the time for me to make you scream!"

"Can you think of a better way to die?" she countered.

Gavir stopped. Looked at her. Shook his head and started laughing. "When you put it that way. Up on the bench, woman. Sitting, facing me, knees apart."

Iras clambered up onto the bench, getting into position, watching him eagerly. Gavir got up onto his knees, moving into place between her legs and resting his hands on her knees. "I wish I had the time to do this properly," he said. "I don't."

"How long would it take?" Iras asked. Gavir grinned, rubbing her legs in long, lazy strokes.

"I did this to another Sword once. I kept her on the edge for nearly an hour, and she damn near killed me before it was done."

"An hour?" Iras's voice trembled slightly, and Gavir felt his smile grow broader.

"And I didn't even tie her down." He pushed Iras' legs wider and ducked his head, kissing his way up her inner thigh. He heard her breath catch as he wrapped his arms around her legs, leaning down to kiss the top of her pubes. She shivered, and he felt her legs straining against his arms. He laughed.

"Not until I'm done with you," he murmured, sliding his hands underneath her ass and lifting her. He lowered his head again, and started to slowly trace the edges of her labia with his tongue. She moaned, running her fingers through his hair, pulling hard when he started lapping at her clit. She started to struggle, and he tightened his hold on her legs, listening to her cries grow louder, more frantic, until she was shrieking and thrashing in his arms. That was his signal—he put her back down on the seat, setting her close to the edge, and rose up on his knees.

She came as he pushed into her, wrapping her legs around his waist and pulling him deeper. He braced himself on the seat and started grinding against her, the only movement he could manage until she let her legs fall. Once she did, he started pumping, long, slow thrusts that left her limp and whimpering, building to another climax. Gavir took a long breath and reached between their bodies, finding her clit with his thumb. This time, she didn't scream—she went rigid, and her cunt clamped down around him like a fist. He howled as he came, slamming hard against her until he couldn't move any more and slumped over her, gasping.

When he could finally breathe again, he pushed himself up and looked at her. Her eyes were closed, and her breathing growing regular. Grinning, he leaned down and kissed her between her breasts.

"I love you, lady-mine," he said, his voice rough.

Iras chuckled softly and opened her eyes. "I love you, too. An hour? Like that?"

Gavir nodded, trying not to laugh. "She damn near killed me. Once she could see straight."

"I can understand that. What I don't understand is why she didn't marry you." Iras sat up slowly, then leaned forward and caught Gavir's face between her hands. She kissed him hungrily, then wrapped her arms around his neck and held on tight. Gavir held her close, rubbing her back with one hand.

"We need to get dressed," he said softly. "Before they come looking for us."

"I know. Just give me a moment." Iras snuggled closer, her head on his shoulder. He let her be, until at last she sighed and pulled away. "All right. Let's get dressed."

Gavir dressed slowly, trying to put off the inevitable. But there was no way to stop it, and he finally he climbed back into the driver's seat and looked across at Iras, already strapped into the passenger seat.

"Ready?" he asked.

"No."

"Are we going anyway?"

She blinked quickly, looked away, then nodded. He smiled and reached out to take her hand.

He didn't need two hands to drive anyway.

Chapter Eight

They entered the Gap without incident, although Iras kept a close watch on the proximity scanners. As they'd approached, Gavir had finally let go of her hand, and he was studying his controls with a fierce intensity.

"Something?" she asked quietly.

"Nothing." He glanced at her, an almost hopeful look on his face. "Maybe they gave up and went home?" He snorted and looked back at the controls. "I could wish."

"Shouldn't we have seen something by now?"

"Yes. That's what's worrying me." Gavir guided the 'car higher, skimming over the top of the rocky chasm that ran from Aakar to Tyese. "If I get enough height, they won't shoot us down. I hope. They want you alive, at least."

Iras looked down at the gun in her lap. "They won't have me."

"I know, love." Gavir said, his voice somber. They'd discussed this at length over the past hour. He knew what she wanted. Knew, and disliked it. "If I can get you alive into Maryst, I will."

"Not without you," Iras repeated.

Gavir sighed. "And if I can't... then we'll die together. I promised."

"Thank you." Iras looked down at the screen, then frowned. "Gavir, there's something here."

"Send it to my forward screen."

Iras flicked her finger over the screen, and the image appeared, ghostly on the window in front of Gavir. He studied it for a moment, then nodded. Iras cleared the screen. "What is that?" she asked.

"A squad carrier. Carries a dozen men or so. I'm willing to bet that's my squad on board, since Demarti is up to his ears in this."

"Is that good or bad?"

"Depends." Gavir scowled. "Some of my men are fiercely loyal to me. The ones that I've served with since my cadet squad. Some... aren't. They see me as an obstacle in the way of their advancement."

"Like Demarti?"

"Like Demarti. He isn't a ranking officer, but he is... charismatic. Men follow him. And when the smoke clears, they ask themselves what the fuck they were doing."

Iras looked down at her screen. "Is there a way to avoid them?"

"Considering they've probably been watching us for the past half an hour? No. This is it, love." Gavir looked over at her. "I love you. I wish we had more time."

"I love you, too. Thank you, for what time we've had."

Gavir smiled at her, reaching out and taking her hand. He kissed her palm, then let her go and put both hands back on the controls. "All right. Let's see how close we can get to Maryst."

To Iras' surprise, there was no movement from the carrier; it remained stationary, hovering outside of the walls of the Neutral City as Gavir landed the aircar in the well-lit clearing near the gatehouse.

"All right. Remember what I told you?" Gavir asked.

"Once we're in the gatehouse, they can't touch us," Iras answered. Gavir nodded, drew his gun and looked at her, arching one eyebrow. Iras nodded and continued, "If anyone gets in our way, go through them. Your gun is set to stun. So is mine. We're not killing anyone. If we do, the Gatekeeper will refuse us entry."

"Good. On three, we run for it. Three... two... go!" He threw open his door and started running, and Iras scrambled after him. She wasn't sure if he'd slowed his pace so she could keep up with him, or if she really was as fast as he was, but they ran side by side across the clearing. Iras allowed herself a brief glance over her shoulder, but could see nothing outside the circle of lights. Looking forward showed they were halfway to the gatehouse. The door ahead of them opened... and two Swords walked out. Gavir skidded to a stop, grabbing Iras' arm.

"Back... back to the 'car..." he said, turning. He froze; Iras turned, and moaned softly, seeing now what the darkness had hidden. There were more Swords between them and the car.

"To the gate?" she whispered.

Gavir nodded once. Then he turned and charged forward, towards the gate. Iras could see now that he'd been holding back—he easily outpaced her, even though she was running as fast as she could. She heard guns firing, saw a flash from ahead of them, then saw Gavir jerk and slow in front of her. He growled, loud enough that she heard him, and kept on going, firing once. One of the Swords fell back. The other—and now Iras was close enough to see that it was Demarti—fired again. Gavir stumbled, falling to one knee. He tried to get up and fell forward. Iras hesitated, then ran to him, grabbing his arm and trying to drag him back to his feet, succeeding only in rolling him onto his back. There were no burns on his clothes, no blood, but the left side of his body was limp.

".. sorry..." he slurred. "..'m... 'm sorry... run..."

"I'm not leaving you," Iras said. She looked at the gun that she still held in one hand, then shook her head, taking Gavir's right hand in hers. He squeezed her fingers, then jerked at the sound of footsteps, coming closer. Iras looked up to see Demarti standing over them.

"Well, my Lady Red. I'd say it was a pleasure, but..." he smiled, looking down at Gavir. Demarti sneered, then spat, the glob landing on the front of Gavir's coat. "Actually, it is truly a pleasure." He raised his voice. "Take her. Secure her in the carrier while I deal with the rogue."

"Deal... what do you mean, deal with the rogue?" Iras asked. She heard more footsteps, coming closer. "What do you mean?"

"Rogue Swords are broken, Lady Red. Executed, by orders of the Council," Demarti answered. "Since he was a freak already, I don't suppose anyone will miss—"

He never had a chance to finish; Iras brought her gun up and fired. At such close range, the stun blast knocked Demarti over backwards, and he dropped like a stone. There was a moment of silence, broken by a rusty, wheezing sound. Iras had just realized that it was Gavir, laughing, when something hit her in the back, knocking her forward into darkness.

⸺◉⸺

"YOU SHOT A CIVILIAN, in the back. A woman that you were charged with bringing safely to me. Have you lost your senses? Or is Demarti's sheer idiocy catching these days?"

Iras vaguely knew the voice, and the tone... well, she hoped she'd never hear that level of derision focused at her. She'd want to curl up and die...

Gavir. Where was Gavir? She groaned and forced her eyes open, only to find herself staring at a stark, white ceiling. Where was she?

"She's waking. You're dismissed. Consider yourself on punishment detail until I forget you exist." That voice again. "Lady Sirase?" The derision was gone, and now she heard only concern. She blinked and turned towards the voice, immediately wishing that she hadn't. Her head felt like someone had used it to hammer dull nails into ferro-cement. A heavy hand patted her arm, and she felt a sharp pinprick in her other arm, followed by receding footsteps.. "Try not to move. Close range stun blasts can cause a bitch of a headache. Once that shot takes hold, you'll feel better."

"Where's Gavir?" she forced herself to ask.

"Three beds over, and under sedation."

Iras blinked again, then managed to turn enough to see the owner of the voice. "Ran-ti-ar. Where am I?"

"You are in the Ishkarin medical facility in Niran City. And I apologize for your treatment, Lady Sirase. It was not our intention."

"My name is Iras," she whispered. "And Gavir explained."

"Did he?" Quaran looked amused. "There are days when I'm glad to have at least one Sword who thinks. I wish more of them did, or we'd never be in this situation. Now... well, Demarti is on his way to the camps. He should never have fired on Gavir, or turned on him without an order from me. Unfortunately, I can't start an investigation in how he got the override codes for Gavir's wrist-comp, or how he got the squad carrier without my clearance. Yet. That would be tantamount to admitting that I ordered Gavir to steal you away."

"Which you can't do. Not without damaging the Council's trust in the Ishkarin," Iras said. She sat up slowly and looked around, pleased that her head didn't fall off. Whatever had been in that injection was starting to work. Not that there was much to see. There was a curtain around her bed, hiding her view of the rest of the room. "Now what?" she asked.

"Now? Well, the Council knows we have you. And they're demanding I hand you over."

"Quaran, please—"

"Iras, do you trust me?" Quaran interrupted. The question was so startlingly like the one Gavir had asked her—how long ago?—that Iras stopped. She licked her lips, looked at him, then answered.

"I don't know. Should I?"

He smiled, a wolf in black synth-leather. "Right now, do you have a choice?"

"I... suppose not."

"Then trust me. If we can save the Creator's daughter, we will." Quaran sighed and leaned back in his chair. "I've put them off for a day and a half, by the by."

"That long? How?"

"Told them that you are apparently one of those people who can't take a stun blast without taking some damage. And that you spent a good portion of yesterday in regen."

Iras frowned. "And... was that true? I don't feel like I was in regen."

"No, but our medic will swear you were there." Quaran winked, and Iras felt herself relax.

"And... Gavir?"

Quaran sobered and looked away. After a moment, he sighed. "Gavir... is one of those people. He's in bad shape, Iras."

"And he can't do regen. How badly hurt is he?"

"He told you that?" Quaran asked, sounding shocked. "He usually plays that card close to his chest. It's not something we want to get out. Bad enough that his squad knew about his problem with stunners."

"Twice. Demarti shot him twice."

"And he got caught in the blast that hit you," Quaran said. "That's why he's sedated. He's in a lot of pain right now. I'm hoping that I don't have to retire him—"

"Oh, you can't!"

"I don't want to," Quaran assured her. "I'm hoping he'll recover. He's a damned fine officer."

"Is he your son?" Iras blurted out. She covered her mouth with her hand, knowing she'd gone too far. Quaran simply shook his head gave her a rueful look.

"Oh, you've heard those rumors? No, Iras. I'm not his father. I sometimes wish he was. Then I wish Felana had kept better track of her partners, so we could have had another of his caliber. But no, he's not mine," Quaran answered. "Do you remember when you served me in the Arena, Iras? Lurana, my former Kian-ti-os, was with me. We shared you and... oh, I must be getting old. What was his name?"

"Sajani. I remember."

"Yes, that's right. Sajani," Quaran added. "Lurana had you, and I had Sajani. Because I don't sleep with women. I'll play with them in the Arena, yes. Especially when there is one who can take as brutal a beating as you can. But for more intimate pleasure, I prefer a man." Quaran laughed. "And Sajani was a sweet lad. He's married now, isn't he?"

"Yes. The day after he left the Arena, he married a girl from his home village. And yes, he is very sweet." Iras drew her knees to her chest. "Now what happens, Ran-ti-ar?"

"Now? I've put them off as long as I can. You'll be handed over to the Council in an hour. There's nothing I can do to stop them." Quaran leaned forward, his elbows on his knees. "Gavir tells me that you deny the contract?"

"There never was a contract that I know of. I was seventeen. I couldn't legally sign anything. My aunt and Timaron were going to make me marry. They told me that law says that they could, that Aunt Destia could sign me over to him as his wife," Iras said. "I ran that night. I never signed the papers. I don't know if Destia did, but we weren't supposed to until the next day, and by then Sirase was supposed to be dead. I signed a contract at the Arena as soon as I legally could."

Quaran nodded. "You know that Timaron has produced a signed marriage contract?"

Iras stiffened. "If I go with him, he'll kill me," she said softly. "Like his other wives."

"There was never any proof of that—"

"I know." Iras hugged her legs and looked away. "Just like there was never any proof of how much he stole from the camps, or how much money he made from the war."

"So what will you do?" Quaran asked.

"I..." Iras stopped. She looked down at her hands. "I'll say goodbye to Gavir. Then... I don't know. What happens to Gavir now?"

Quaran frowned. "I'm not sure I understand."

"He... you're not going to send him to the camps, are you?" Iras asked. "Please, please, don't do that. Don't... he was following your orders, he told me. Even thought they went wrong, they were still your orders!"

"And I've no intention of sending him anywhere, my dear," Quaran said gently. "You feel strongly about this."

"I love him," Iras said in a whisper. "And... thank you. I'll sleep better, knowing he's not going to be punished for helping me. I... I want to say goodbye to him."

"All right. I'll leave you to do that. I don't know how much he'll hear."

"I'll still know I said it." Iras untangled herself from the light blanket covering her legs and got to her feet. She wobbled slightly, and Quaran caught her arm and steadied her.

"This way, Iras," Quaran said. He kept a hand on her arm as he escorted her around the barrier and towards the bed where Gavir lay, silent and still, his breathing slow and regular. His chest was bare, and she could see angry-looking red burns marring his skin, accentuated by a shiny gel.

"Healing gel," Quaran said. He helped her to sit, then patted her shoulder and walked away. She waited until she could no longer hear his footsteps, then took Gavir's limp hand in hers.

"I'm sorry," she said softly. "I'm so very sorry. I don't know if you can hear me, but thank you, for trying to save me. For loving me. I do love you, and I wish we had longer. I will treasure the time we had, for as long as I live. And... if he kills me... avenge me, please?" She swallowed, unable to say anything else. She slowly stood up, laying his hand down at his side before leaning down to kiss his lips. Then she walked away.

⇒●⇐

QUARAN CAME BACK INTO the infirmary and walked down to stand at the foot of the only occupied bed. He kicked the foot of the bed.

"You can stop playing dead now."

"Which brings up the question of just why I needed to play dead?" Gavir asked, opening his eyes. "I'd have liked to say goodbye without worrying her. She's got enough to deal with."

"Because I needed to hear her. Now, we've got exactly no time. You up to working, Gavir?"

Gavir grimaced as he sat up. "I'm up for saving my Iras' life. Where am I going?"

"You are finding out what happened to Timaron's wives."

Chapter Nine

Iras sat silently in the antechamber, listening to the bustling of the attendant assigned to her. They had brought fresh clothing so that she could change out of her dirty, rumpled clothing, and plied her with food and drink. She ignored their efforts, only speaking when another attendant had come in and announced that Destia wished to speak to her niece.

"I won't see her," Iras said. "Send her away."

"But, ma'am—"

"I said no." Iras turned and looked at the attendant. "I will not see her. She'll see me soon enough in the Council chamber."

After that, Iras was left alone, until at last a uniformed guard came in, bowed slightly, and held out one hand.

"It's time, my lady."

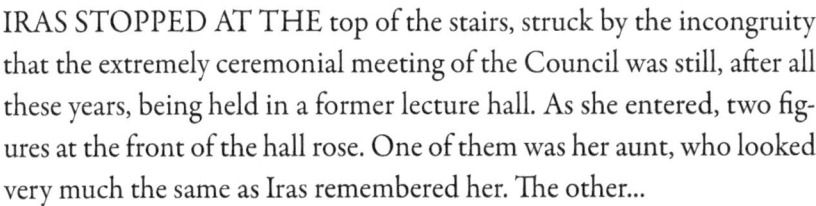

IRAS STOPPED AT THE top of the stairs, struck by the incongruity that the extremely ceremonial meeting of the Council was still, after all these years, being held in a former lecture hall. As she entered, two figures at the front of the hall rose. One of them was her aunt, who looked very much the same as Iras remembered her. The other...

Timaron had lost weight since she'd seen him last. His clothing was new and very fashionable, and Iras had no doubt that the tasteful jewelry he was wearing was real. He looked every inch the prosperous merchant he claimed to be, and she wondered where the money had come from this time. She looked away from him, following the guard to a seat at the front of the hall, where she found herself standing next to Chief

Administrator Brinnock. He nodded at her, but didn't smile. She remained standing as the Council filed in and took their places.

"The Council is assembled," Andradae announced. "Who comes before us?"

"I do," Timaron announced. "I am Timaron a'Granion, and I have come to ask the Council to enforce the law, and a contract that has remained unfulfilled since the signing. I hold that my lady wife, Sirase a'Mathias, violated the terms of our contract by abandoning her marital duties. Further, I hold that her terms of indenture in the Arena were entered into fraudulently, and as such, her earnings from that period are forfeit."

"Forfeit to you?" one of the Councilors asked.

"I should think that fair. Both as recompense for the abandonment, and to address the anguish of believing myself a widower for over five years, when in truth my wife was alive and living a false life as a whore."

"I am not a whore!" Iras snapped.

"You will have your say in a moment," Andradae said gently. She glared at Timaron. "There is no need to be insulting, Timaron. Those who wear the collar are more than... sexual servants."

"You make it sound so genteel," Timaron sneered. "She's spent five years spreading her legs for every Sword who beckoned to her, debasing her own name and. because of our union, mine. I demand recompense for that insult."

Iras stood and listened to Timaron's insulting rant, seething silently and trying to hide her anger. Serving the Arena was an honor, one that was highly sought after, and not just because of the rewards waiting after the contract was fulfilled. Chief Administrator Brinnock looked equally angry, but he said nothing.

"Sirase a'Mathias—"

"Iras Taramar," Iras corrected. "Sirase a'Mathias is dead."

"Very well. Iras Taramar, what say you?"

"I deny the contract. When he and my aunt attempted to force me to marry, I was under the legal age. I refused the marriage, and I signed my contract at the Arena the day I turned eighteen." Iras shook her head. "I did not want the marriage, and I still do not want it. In any case, I signed my contract with the Arena on my eighteenth birthday." She kept silent her fears about how short her life would be if forced to marry Timaron—the rumors were still just that. There had never been any proof—

"I have a copy of that contract," Brinnock added. He handed a datapad to a guard, who carried it up to the Council. Andradae took the 'pad and set it aside.

"Timaron has also presented a contract signed by you and by your guardian." Andradae picked up a scroll and handed it to a guard, who carried it to Iras. She unrolled it, and found herself looking at her aunt's signature, and under it, her own. She shook her head again.

"Impossible. I never signed this!"

"Is that your signature?"

"It appears to be," Iras admitted. "Although I swear to you, I did not sign this." She looked at the contract again, and her heart leapt. "But look here. The date on this contract is the day after I ran away. By that time, Sirase a'Mathias was legally dead. Who would sign a contract to marry a dead woman? And how can one sign a contract?" She glanced at Timaron, who glared at her, then at Destia. That was when Iras knew.

"You forgot the day I died, didn't you, Aunt?" she asked. "You put the wrong date on this—"

"Senior Councilor, I protest!" Timaron interrupted. "There was an agreement to marry! The contract had been draw up, and it was signed by Destia a'Arthian, Sirase's legal guardian. There was the assurance that it would be honored! Surely—"

The doors at the rear of the hall slammed open, making Iras jump. She turned to see a wall of black-clad figures coming towards the front of the room. Her heart stuttered in her chest—there, behind Quaran, limping slightly and still far too pale, was Gavir. He caught her looking at him and winked.

"Quaran, what is the meaning of this?" Andradae demanded, rising from her chair.

"We beg your indulgence, Senior Councilor," Quaran answered. "But we've come for one of our own." Moving in a dark wave, the Ishkarin formed a semi-circle around Iras. She felt a warm hand on her back, and looked up to see Gavir at her side.

"This... are these abominations going to be allowed to... to desecrate these proceedings?" Timaron sputtered.

"Desecrate? That's a fine word, coming from you," Gavir called out. He moved from Iras' side and held out his hand. Quaran handed him a data-pad, and Gavir carried it towards the Councilors. "Senior Councilor, what do you know of Timaron's previous marriages?"

Andradae frowned, taking the 'pad. "Only that he was wed. Unless you refer to the rumors, in which case, I'd ask you for proof."

"Which you now hold," Gavir said. He bowed slightly and backed away from the table before turning and looking at Timaron. "When you buy someone, murderer, make certain that they stay bought. The examiner who swore that your wives died in childbirth kept excellent personal records that he was willing to share with us. Records that showed the lethal levels of Aakari fedelis nectar in the blood of each of those poor ladies."

"Lies!"

"We thought you would say that, Timaron," Quaran called out. "So we had them exhumed—"

"Ran-ti-ar, this is unheard of!" Andradae interrupted. "Without Council permission?"

"I chose rather to seek forgiveness," Quaran answered. "As permission might very well have cost the Creator's daughter her life. The records of the examination of the bodies is also on the 'pad."

Andradae frowned, her fingers moving over the screen. Her eyes flickered up, looking at Timaron, then back down.

"This meeting will be adjourned," she said without looking up. "Until such time as this new... evidence has been examined and the veracity determined."

"But the contract—!"

"A verbal contract is not binding, Timaron. And, as has been pointed out, your contract was signed after the intended bride was legally dead. Which raises the question of how she signed it? Or was it signed for her? And... I wonder. When would the records hall would show this contract was filed?" Andradae looked at Timaron, her face cold. "Your suit is dismissed. And in addition..." Andradae frowned and looked down at the scroll, then at the datapad that Brinnock had given to her. "The Council rules that this attempt at coercion is unlawful. You, Timaron, will be charged with perjury and fraud. As will you, Destia a'Arthian." Andradae smiled, and Timaron turned pale.

"I... I plead ignorance, Senior Councilor," Timaron stammered.

"It was your idea!" Destia screamed. "Your plan, to rid me of the damned girl!"

"Oh, there's a confession," Quaran muttered. "But it's none of our concern. Not now."

"Now, before we adjourn, there is the matter of Iras Taramar's identity to address. Iras, come forward," Andradae added. Iras swallowed and nodded, stepping forward.

"Senior Councilor?"

Andradae looked amused. "This may be the first time I have ever asked this question, but who do you wish to be? If you wish, we can reinstate your identity as Sirase a'Mathias, and restore your caste and your estate."

Iras didn't even have to think about it. "No. I am Iras, Senior Councilor. I..." Iras hesitated, then felt strong hands on her shoulders.

"And if she is willing, she will be Iras, wife of Gavir Kian-ti-os," Gavir said, his voice carrying to every corner of the room. Iras looked up at him and nodded.

"Yes. Yes, that is my answer," she answered without looking away from Gavir.

"Very well," Andradae said with a smile. "The Arena's loss in the Ishkarin's gain. There is the matter of the a'Mathias estate—"

"There's something left?" Iras blurted. She felt her face grow warm. "Oh, I apologize. I just... Aunt Destia was... ah... profligate with my allowances."

"On your death," Andradae's lips quirked as she spoke. "Your fortune was placed into a trust for the benefit of female refugees and survivors of the war. You didn't know that your father's will had that provision?"

"No, Senior Councilor!" Iras gasped. "And... I'd like that to stay the way it is. Let the money do some good. I've no need of it, and... it's what I'd do anyway. What I always wanted for myself, but my aunt kept me from doing publicly." She looked over her shoulder at Gavir, who smiled. "And... could something be done to change that law? The one that allows a minor's guardian to sell them into a marriage contract?"

Andradae nodded. "It's an archaic law. We should overturn it, to allow new growth. Consider it done. Good luck, Iras. And congratulations."

"Thank you." Iras turned and walked away, walked straight into Gavir's arms. He pulled her close, and she could feel his breath on her neck.

"Not too tight, love," he murmured into her ear. "I'm one long ache."

"I'm shocked to see you on your feet," Iras answered. "Are you all right?"

He pulled back and smiled at her. "I'll be fine. I'm assured that I'll have an excellent nurse." He stepped back, keeping his arm around her as he started moving, walking towards the doors. Iras let herself relax, sliding her arm around his back as they walked. She was safe.

"Sirase?"

Iras stopped, turning at the sound of her aunt's voice. She hadn't realized that Destia had followed them. This close, Iras could see that Destia was apparently holding on to her youthful appearance with tooth, claw and cosmetic brush—her hair had been badly dyed, and her cosmetics were applied thickly enough that it was caking and cracking at the corners of her mouth.

"I've nothing to say to you, Aunt," Iras said, trying hard to keep the contempt out of her voice. "I never want to see you again."

"You never will," Destia said coldly. "You've ruined me."

"You did that to yourself."

"Gavir, please," Iras said, resting her hand on his chest. He looked at her, met her eyes, then nodded. Iras turned back to her aunt and shook her head. "Goodbye, Destia."

She turned away, hearing Destia behind her saying, "Goodbye, Sirase." There was a shout from one of the other Swords—"Gun!" Then Iras was on the ground, something heavy pinning her down, her ears ringing from twin explosions. A woman was screaming—Destia? Iras struggled and squirmed out from underneath the weight pinning her down, and realized when it groaned that it was Gavir.

"Gavir?" she gasped, pushing him until he'd rolled onto his back. That was when she saw the blood. "Gavir!"

"Medic! We need a medic!" Someone was shouting. Iras didn't know who. She didn't care. She tore open Gavir's coat, finding more blood, a gaping wound in his chest. Someone dropped down on Gavir's other side, pressing something cloth into the wound and holding it there.

"Marauder pistol," Quaran said without looking at her. "Single shot job, all plastics. Never set off the alarms. Blew up in her hand, the damned fool. Hold this, here." He waited until Iras had started pressing on the makeshift compress, then reached up and slapped Gavir's face. "Stay with us, boy!"

"...hear... I... I hear..." Gavir muttered. "Not... not... dead.... yet."

"Not dying, damn it all!" Iras snapped. "Don't you dare!"

Gavir let out a weak snort. "No... no, ma'am. Try... not... " He stopped, swallowed. Coughed, and Iras saw the blood on his lips. So did Quaran.

"Where's that damned medic!"

Chapter Ten

The corridor was full of men and women in black uniforms milling around and talking in low voices. Every so often, one of them would come and ask Iras if she needed anything—a drink, something to eat, someone to talk to—until Iras lost her patience and her temper and screamed at all of them to just leave her alone.

"They mean well, Iras," Quaran said softly as he came and sat down next to her. "They just... well, you're new. They don't know how to treat you."

"New?" Iras repeated. "I've served more than half of them in the Arena."

"And you're marrying a Sword. No one from outside our ranks has done that before. They don't know how to treat you, especially since you have served more than half of them. Now you're the Kian-ti-os' lady, and they don't have a framework."

Iras considered it, then nodded. "All right. I'll apologize. Later. Have you heard anything?"

"Nothing yet. Which I should think is a good thing." Quaran leaned back and sighed. "She's dead, by the by. If you care."

"I don't, but thank you."

"I just regret I didn't get to kill her myself," Quaran said.

Iras looked at him.

"That's my boy in there," Quaran continued, shaking his head. "Closest thing I'll ever have to a son. I watched him grow to be the finest officer in the Ishkarin. He survived the war, and the rebuilding. He cannot die like this."

"He won't," Iras said. She took Quaran's hand in hers and squeezed tightly. "He'll be fine."

"He's got a lot to live for," another man said from behind Iras. She turned to face a familiar older man, who smiled gently and patted her shoulder. "Doubt you remember me. I'm Delan. He'll pull through. And we'll all be here to help him."

"All?" The word reminded Iras of something, and she looked up and down the hall. "What about Demarti?"

"That little piss is screaming his head off in solitary confinement in the internment camps," Delan answered. "Insubordination is the mildest charge he's facing."

"And how did he get the override codes?"

Quaran scowled. "He seduced one of the programmers who work in Ishkarin control. She told him everything, and kept it off my screens. She damn near cut me out of the loop entirely. I'd no idea there was a search on until Delan discovered it. Which reminds me. Delan, we need to see who among the trainees up north might have the aptitude to take over those positions? A Sword wouldn't have turned on Gavir the way that bitch did."

Iras refrained from pointing out that a Sword had turned on Gavir, but Delan didn't.

"Oh, so Demarti isn't a Sword?"

"Delan—"

"You know what they've been saying, Quaran. We all know. Gavir's had a target painted on his back since he tested. And you know why."

"I know," Quaran agreed.

"I don't," Iras said. "And I'm not entirely sure Gavir does. He told me that there are those who think he's a freak. He called himself a blunted Sword—" A low growl from all around cut off anything else Iras was going to say.

"You'll find that is not the popular opinion, Iras," Quaran said. "There's a undercurrent that we're working to root out, an... elitist thread that runs through the Ishkarin. Swords that believe that weakness is a failing, that compassion is a major fault. That fine men like

Gavir or Delan are defective, and should be removed from the breeding pool before they contaminate it. They think I sold them out, that they should have been allowed to prey on the people and rule the known world. And they intend to win back what they think I stole from them. Gavir's not the only target. There have been five attempts on my life in the last six months."

"That's horrible! And Demarti was a part of that group?"

"It appears so," Quaran answered. He sighed and slipped his hand out of Iras'. "Now, I'm going to stretch my legs. Should I risk asking you if you want anything, or will you scream at me, too?"

Iras smiled slightly and was about to answer when she was someone in white moving amongst the black. She stiffened, her heart pounding in her ears. "Quaran..."

He turned and rose, holding his hand out to Iras. She took it, standing beside him as older woman in a medic's uniform came towards them. "Ran-ti-ar?"

"Yes. How is Gavir?"

"Well, it was touch-and-go for a while, what with not being able to use regen therapy. We had to find someone who knew how to do the surgery," the medic said, her face serious. "But he is strong, and he's responding well. We're reasonably certain that he'll pull through."

Iras felt her legs buckle, then Quaran's strong arm around her, keeping her on her feet. "When can I see him?" she asked.

"He's still under sedation," the medic said. "He won't be awake for hours yet."

"I don't care. I just want to see him."

"This is Gavir's wife," Quaran told the medic. Iras looked at him, and he shook his head slightly.

"Oh! Oh, I'd no idea. I apologize, my lady. If you'll come with me?"

She found her feet and followed the medic, hearing Quaran behind her, hearing Delan's voice fading in the distance as he told the other

Swords to go home, that their Kian-ti-os was going to be fine. There was a ragged, muted cheer, cut off as she and Quaran went through a door.

"This way, please," the medic said. She stopped outside a door and looked at them. "I will warn you, it's not pretty. He lost a lot of blood, and the damage was extensive. He'll be in recovery for quite some time."

"But he will recover," Iras said softly. "That's the important part."

"If he listens and does what he's told, and doesn't rush, then yes, he should recover. He'll have interesting scars—"

"We all have interesting scars," Quaran said drily. "Thank you."

"If you need anything, press the call button on the wall and ask for me. My name is Kilani," the medic said. She held the door open for them, and Quaran let Iras enter first.

The room was dimly lit, and filled with muted sounds coming from the machines that surrounded the bed. "I haven't seen equipment like this since I was a boy," Quaran murmured. Iras ignored him, looking at the silent, pale figure laying on the bed. A respirator mask concealed the lower part of his face, and it seemed that there were wires and tubes everywhere.

"How long did she say?" Iras asked without turning.

"A few hours."

"Well, then." She moved over to one side of the bed and looked at Quaran. "We'll need some chairs."

———————⬧———————

THE COMBINATION OF too much stress, too much drama, and general lack of sleep led to Iras dozing in her chair, leaning over the side of Gavir's bed with her head on her pillowed arms, her right hand resting on Gavir's forearm. When he moved, she jumped, looking up to see him looking confused, his eyes darting from side to side.

"Gavir?" He focused on her, and the tension in his arm faded. But the furrow between his brows remained. She smiled and squeezed his arm. "You're in the medical center. It's all right."

The furrow deepened, and Iras shook her head. "No, I'm not sure what happened. It all happened too fast."

"Well, look who woke up." Quaran came up behind Iras and rested his hand on her shoulder. "Welcome back. You gave us all a fright, Gavir."

"Quaran, what exactly did happen?" Iras asked. "I never asked, and Gavir wants to know."

"That woman... she must have known something was going to go wrong. She brought a pistol... and calling that piece of garbage a pistol is insulting. It was a one-shot wonder, Gavir. The kind of weapon morons use in back-room brawls and turf warfare. She was going to kill Iras. And you stepped in front of the shot." He reached out and patted Gavir's leg. "Idiot."

The growl was audible, even past the respirator mask. Quaran laughed. "Yes, you are an idiot! She can take regen, and you can't!"

"Quaran, it doesn't matter," Iras said, taking Gavir's hand in hers. "He'll be fine. I'll make sure of it." She smiled as Gavir squeezed her fingers gently. "I will have to go out, for an hour or two."

The furrow was back between Gavir's brows, but it was Quaran who asked the question. "Go where?"

"The Arena," Iras answered. She reached up and touched her collar. "I need to return this." She met Gavir's eyes and he nodded. "And I need to see the Arena medics." She looked over her shoulder at Quaran. "That... is personal."

"Iras, give me some credit for intelligence, will you?" Quaran said, looking as if he wanted to laugh. "I know that Collared have their fertility offset during their time of service."

Gavir squeezed Iras' fingers again. She looked at him, then leaned over and kissed his forehead. "Yes, love. I love you."

She heard a hiss, and looked up to see one of the lights on a monitor blinking. When she looked back down, Gavir's eyes were closed.

"Probably a pain-killer," Quaran offered. "He'll sleep more than he's awake for a few days."

"Will you stay with him, while I'm gone?" Iras asked. She rose, and Quaran took her seat.

"Yes," he answered. "But you'd better hurry back. If he wakes up before you get back, I'm not guaranteeing I can keep him in that bed."

Iras laughed. She kissed Quaran's cheek, then hurried from the room, her hands already working at the buckle at the back of her neck.

At long last, she was free.

About the Author

Elizabeth Schechter has been called one of the top erotica and alternative sexuality writers in the world. Her writing credits include the award-winning steampunk erotic romance *House of Sable Locks* and the Celtic fantasy *Princes of Air*. Her shorter work has appeared in anthologies edited by D.L King (*Carnal Machines*), Laura Antoniou (*No Safewords*), and Cecilia Tan (*Jingle Balls; Like a Prince*). Elizabeth Schechter was born in New York at some point in the past. She is officially old enough to know better, but refuses to grow up. She lives in Central Florida with her husband and son, and a most accepting circle of friends who are both very amused and very proud of the pervy, fetish writer in their midst. Elizabeth can be found online at http://elizabethschechterwrites.com[1] or at https://www.facebook.com/Elizabeth.A.Schechter.

---

1. http://elizabethschechterwrites.com/

More from award-winning author Elizabeth Schechter

Playing for Keeps

A novel in the *Tales from the Arena* series!
Rakesh is one of the most skilled of the Collared. Virin, a mid-ranking sword, takes Rakesh as his lover and hopes to rise high enough in rank that they may marry. But a storm is brewing. Former Collareds are disappearing, victims of a dark conspiracy of renegade soldiers that conspires to utterly control the nation of Tyrese and destroy all who oppose them. And they have their eyes on Rakesh.

Heart's Master

by Elizabeth Schechter

In one tragic night Steven loses everything: his lover, his dreams, and his sight, but he gains the compassionate, caring dominant he has always longed for. Nick must teach Steven not only how to have a healthy and consensual BDSM relationship, but how to navigate the ways of magic. But as Steven begins to wield his new--and terrifyingly strong--powers, he draws the attention of evil beyond our world.

House of Sable Locks

by Elizabeth Schechter

Winner of the Passionate Plume Award

A steampunk novel of dark passion. Dominant and implacable, the Succubus is all that men crave and fear. However, she has met her match in William, a young aristocrat trained to be the perfect submissive. Their idyll cannot last: there is a killer loose in London, and William's dark past is about to collide with the present.

All Genres ⊆┼ All Genders

⊆┼Circlet Press: Erotica For Geeks www.circlet.com

If you enjoyed this book, you might also enjoy...

Superlative Speculative Erotica
edited by Cecilia Tan and Bethany Zaiatz
Twenty of the best erotic science fiction and fantasy stories published by Circlet Presson our 25th anniversary. A little cyberpunk, some high fantasy, a touch of horror, some superheroes, a bit of space opera, some paranormal... What unites these stories is their quality. The anthology also features characters who identify as lesbian, gay, genderqueer, bisexual, trans, and heterosexual. What label do you put on a book like that? We call it... superlative speculative erotica.

Fantastic Erotica
edited by Cecilia Tan & Bethany Zaiatz
To celebrate the 20th Anniversary of Circlet Press, Fantastic Erotica presents the very best erotic science fiction and fantasy short stories published by Circlet in the past five years. Chosen by popular vote by the readership from among all the stories published by Circlet from 2008 to the present, these favorites are the cream of the crop.

Best Fantastic Erotica
edited by Cecilia Tan
The best erotic science fiction and fantasy as determined by the annual contest run by Circlet Press. Rewarding originality and positive sensuality, the contest inspires well-known and unknown writers alike to excel in this provocative genre. Erotic sf/f combines erotic and sexual themes with magic, futurism, high fantasy, cyberpunk, space opera, magic realism, and all the many other sub-genres.

All Genres ☾ All Genders

☾ Circlet Press: Erotica For Geeks www.circlet.com

About the Publisher

Circlet Press: Erotica for Geeks. All genres, all genders. Circlet Press has been publishing fine quality erotic science fiction, fantasy, and genre literature since 1992. We love a good sexy story, well told, that sparks the imagination.